STEEPLECHASE

Other Homer Kelly mysteries by Jane Langton

Jane Langton

STEEPLECHASE

THOMAS DUNNE BOOKS

ST. MARTIN'S MINOTAUR

NEW YORK

1811

THOMAS DUNNE BOOKS.
An imprint of St. Martin's Press.

STEEPLECHASE. Copyright © 2005 by Jane Langton. Illustrations © 2005 by Jane Langton. All rights reserved. Printed in the United States of America. No part of this book may be used or reproduced in any manner whatsoever without written permission except in the case of brief quotations embodied in critical articles or reviews. For information, address St. Martin's Press, 175 Fifth Avenue, New York, N.Y. 10010.

www.minotaurbooks.com

Design by Phil Mazzone

The photograph on page 25 is number 206 in *The Medical and Surgical History of the War of the Rebellion (1861–1865)*, prepared in accordance with the acts of Congress under the direction of Surgeon General Joseph K. Barnes, U.S. Army, Washington, Government Printing Office, 1870–88.

ISBN 0-312-30195-2
EAN 978-0-312-30195-8

First Edition: November 2005

10   9   8   7   6   5   4   3   2   1

For Joe Gillson

1868

The Aeronauts

Thank God, men cannot as yet fly, and lay waste the sky as well as the earth!

—Henry Thoreau, *Journal*,
January 3, 1861

The Brothers Spratt

The wind was blowing gently west-southwest. Two church steeples in the town of Bedford veered away below the balloon as the Spratt brothers dropped their leaflets, and before long two more spires appeared above the trees in the town of Concord.

"Two churches apiece they got, Jack," said Jake.

"Right you are, Jake," said Jack. "Two apiece."

Looking down, they could see Hector. He was standing up in his wagon, whooping at his tired old horse as it galloped after them along the road.

Now the main street of Concord opened out below them. Pale Concord faces gazed up. Jake slid the lid halfway over the firebox, and the balloon drifted lower over the housetops so that everyone could read the painted words on the bag:

J. & J. SPRATT
PORTRAIT AND AERIAL
PHOTOGRAPHY

Jake picked up another bundle of pamphlets, dropped them over the side, and watched them flutter down on the street. Some lodged on rooftops, some disappeared in the leafy canopies of elm trees, some fell on the muddy road, and some were caught by eager hands reaching up.

"Whoopsie, Jake," said Jack, because the wind was shifting into another quarter.

"Going due west now, Jack," said Jake, and he opened the firebox again to lift the balloon high over the road to Nashoba. As it rose, he leaned out to look for Hector. Had he caught up? Yes, there was the wagon, a speck in the distance, with Hector's old horse pounding along at a gallop.

Jake made a huge pointing gesture—*West, Hector, we're heading west*—and Hector understood. He was waving his hat in the same direction.

"This here must be Nashoba, Jake," said Jack as the next town came in sight.

"Right you are, Jack," said Jake. "Hey, Jack, look at that there big tree."

"What tree, Jake?" said Jack.

"Down there in the graveyard, Jack. See there?"

"My goodness, Jake. I ain't never seen such a big old granddaddy tree."

"Whoopsie, Jack. I almost forgot." Nimbly, Jake untied another packet of pamphlets and dropped them over the side. Once again, hands reached up and children ran after fluttering scraps of paper. Looking back, Jack and Jake saw the main street of Nashoba drifting away behind them, until only the low dome of the church steeple was visible above the trees.

"Wind's died," said Jake. "We'd best go down."

"Where to, Jake? In that there field?"

"See if Hector's a-coming, Jack," said Jake, closing the fire-box.

"Yep, Jake. I see his horse and wagon. That poor old nag, she's weaving all over the road."

"Poor thing must be wore-out," said Jake. "Whoopsie! Hang on, Jack."

The basket settled with a bump in the pasture, tipped, dragged, bounced, tipped, dragged, and at last came to a stop in the grassy stubble between two flabbergasted cows.

NOW

Joy on the River

"Why!" said I . . . "the stones are happy, Concord River is happy, and I am happy too. . . . Do you think that Concord River would have continued to flow these millions of years by Clamshell Hill and round Hunt's Island . . . if it had been miserable in its channel, tired of existence, and cursing its maker and the hour that it sprang?"

—Henry Thoreau, *Journal,*
January 6, 1857

Homer's Happy Day

Something amazing was happening. Homer Kelly had become a star.

"I know it's ridiculous," said his editor. "I mean, it's like a meteor falling on your head. That book of yours is number one on the *Times* bestseller list for nonfiction."

"But Luther, it came out three years ago," crowed Homer happily. "This is just a reprint of a boring old scholarly work. There isn't a ripped bodice in it anywhere."

Luther chuckled. "Well, who knows the ways of Providence? Sometimes it casteth down; sometimes it raiseth up."

"Having often been casteth down," cried Homer, "I'm grateful to be raiseth up."

"Watch it," scolded Luther, who was a stickler for grammatical perfection. "Thou shouldest not mess around with tricky old verb forms like that."

They argued gaily for a while about *eths* and *ests, thees* and *thous,* and then Homer cackled a jolly good-bye. He wanted to jump up and down, but he was afraid the floorboards would snap under his six and a half feet of flab. Instead, he bounded out the door and hollered at his wife, "Number one, I'm number one."

Mary looked up from the shallows, where she was boot-deep in pickerelweed, and shouted back, "That's crazy. It's just ridiculous." But she, too, was laughing as she slopped out of the water.

Homer hurtled down the porch steps and hoisted her off the ground. "You know what a bestselling writer gotta have?" he chortled joyfully. "He gotta have champagne. We'll just make a little trip into town."

It was a happy day. "I deserve it," said Homer smugly, raising his glass. "I've been in the wilderness too long."

"You certainly have," said Mary.

"And the strangest thing has been happening in our department. Have you noticed that all the new grad students are mere babies? The other day, I swear I saw one of them sucking her thumb."

"It's not that they're younger, Homer dear; it's just that we're older. But honestly, this is such a wild stroke of luck. Whatever got into all those people, going into all those stores and buying a book about the spread of old New England churches?"

"I've become chic, that's it," bragged Homer, pouring Mary another glass. "Everybody's got to have my *Hen and Chicks.*"

"They won't read it, of course," said Mary, laughing. "It isn't exactly a page-turner."

"Well, who the hell cares?"

After lunch, Homer hauled the battered aluminum canoe down to the water's edge for a celebratory paddle, but his phone buzzed as he shoved off. He put it to his ear, yelled, "Just a sec," and stuck it in his pocket while he poled the canoe away from the shore. Afloat at last, he pulled out the phone. "Okay, here I am."

It was Luther again, more excited than ever. "Listen, Homer, we've got to follow this up; we've got to strike while the iron is hot. How's the new book coming along?"

The breeze was mild, the river placid. Homer was appalled. "The new book? Christ, Luther, it isn't anywhere near ready. I haven't done the work. I've got to go to all those churches and talk to people."

"I seem to remember it's got a cute title. What is it? I forget."

"Oh God," groaned Homer, seeing the heavy labor of the next few months appear before him like a cloud over the river. "I'm going to call it *Steeplechase.*"

"Oh, right, that's great. *Steeplechase,* meaning chasing around after churches. Really catchy. Well, get to work, Homer. Throw it together. Like I said, we've got to strike while the iron is hot. People will gobble it up, a peek through the keyhole at all the dirty linen hidden away under all those pious steeples. You know what I mean, Homer, an overview."

"An overview?" Homer's voice was hollow.

"The title alone will do the trick. Think of the book clubs; think of the advance sales. An overview, that's all we want, Homer, a godlike view from above." Luther laughed and shouted, "Get to work, Homer. *Steeplechase!* Tarantara!"

1868

A Godlike View from Above

Jack and Jacob Spratt
Aerial and Portrait Photographers
Cartes de visite, cabinet photographs
Men, women, children, and babes
Mortuarie images a specialty

Our mobile studio will be at your service
on the green in Concord
10 o'clock, Sat'y, May 16.
Satisfaction garanteed

Eben

A storm of paper drifted down over Concord's Milldam, flapping all over the road. One pamphlet slapped the nose bag of a horse tied up at the Middlesex Hotel. Startled, it reared and plunged. An astonished deacon plucked another from the front of his coat.

When one of the flying pamphlets drifted lazily back and forth over the head of Eben Flint, he reached up, smiling, and took it out of the air. It wasn't every day that messages fell from the sky. Was this an angelic announcement?

But, of course, it was only a broadside dropped from the hot-air balloon that was majestically disappearing behind the elm trees on Main Street. Eben read the message as he headed for the bank.

"Eben, Eben," called Ella Viles. From across the street, she waved a pamphlet.

Eben waited, watching her dart in front of a team hauling a wagonload of empty barrels. The driver shouted, "Whoa," the heads of the horses jerked back, and the hollow barrels thumped and rattled. Angrily, the driver shouted, "What's your hurry, miss?"

Ella only giggled and bolted to the other side, skipping over puddles in a flurry of swaying skirts. Breathlessly, she held up the pamphlet. "Oh, Eben, we must both be taken."

Against the background of the dull mercantile street, she was a lovely object. Behind her, two ladies in drab shawls were gossiping in front of Cutler's Dry and Fancy Goods, a hired girl hurried past with a basket of eggs, one of the Hosmers shook hands with one of the Wheelers as they agreed to trade two bushels of turnips for one of winter-stored apples, and the fish cart rattled past the town pump, the driver blowing his horn.

Did Eben mind the way Ella teased him about their names being so much alike? Did he mind her inference that it was the hand of Fate? Did he object to the way she kept saying, "Eben and I," "Me and Eben?" No, he didn't mind. Not when it came so sweetly from such a pretty creature as Ella Viles.

As the wagon rumbled away down the Milldam with its wobbling cargo of barrels, Eben smiled at Ella and shook his head. "I don't need another likeness. I've already been taken."

"Oh, that one. I've seen that one. Oh, Eben, you were just a little boy. The war is over, and now that you're back home, you're so much more grown-up and good-looking." Ella blushed and dropped her eyes. "And, oh, Eben, I hope you'll like to have my picture?" Tittering, she said, "My gracious, I'll have to order a whole set, I have so many admirers."

This was said in jest, but it had the desired effect. Eben gazed at her without speaking, and she told herself how delightful it was to be so pretty and to be standing so close to Eben Flint, right here on the Milldam. How that old spinster Betsy Hubble must envy Ella Viles! And surely the other ladies on the street were saying to one another, "There they are again. You always see them together, Ella Viles and Eben Flint."

But then Ella remembered that she had sensational news, and her face turned solemn. She stepped closer and lowered her voice, "Oh, Eben, have you heard about James?"

"James?"

"James Shaw." Ella's eyes shone with the excitement of being the first to tell the horrid story. "He was your teacher, wasn't he, Eben? Your old friend? Oh, Eben, do you mean you haven't heard the dreadful news?"

Eben stiffened and said sharply, "Tell me."

"He's back from that hospital in Philadelphia. And, Eben, they say"—Ella's eyes widened and her voice sank to a whisper— "they say he's dreadfully *disfigured*."

Eben stared at her blankly, and she hurried on. "Oh, poor Isabelle! James was such a catch, remember, Eben? All us girls in school, we were so jealous, but now— Oh, poor Isabelle."

"She's with him?" said Eben. "Isabelle and James are back home in Nashoba?"

"So they say." Ella looked slyly at Eben. "I remember how everybody used to say you were sweet on Isabelle. But now, just imagine what her life will be like, married to that— Oh, poor *dear* Isabelle!"

Horace

Dr. Alexander Clock picked up his bag and looked at his brother-in-law soberly. "I don't know, Eben. I told you, I've seen James and I've seen his wife. She told me James wants no visitors."

"But James was my friend before the war. He was like an older brother." Stubbornly, Eben pulled on his coat. "And I was in school with Isabelle."

"But Eben, it's very bad." Alexander gazed out the open door at the two Miss Rochesters, who were bouncing on the seat of their runabout, racing along the road to Barrett's mill behind their high-stepping mare.

Eben wondered if the Misses Dorothea and Margaret Roch-

ester were scurrying to call on the neighbors and pass along the
sad news about James Shaw. "Do you think I can't bear it?"

"No, it isn't that."

Alexander's wife, Ida, called down from the top of the hall
stairs, "Have you seen Horace?" She hurried down and threw
open the door to the sitting room. "I thought he was still napping, but he's gone again."

At once, Eben bounded away to look in the kitchen, calling for
his nephew, while Alexander shouted, "Horace, where are you?"

But Horace was nowhere in the house. He was out-of-
doors, darting joyfully into the henhouse and astonishing the
chickens. When they flew up and squawked, he ran out again
and romped across a bedsheet that had been spread out on the
grass to bleach in the sun. A tin pail was hanging upside down
on a fence post, and it bonked as Horace scrambled over the
fence. In the pasture, he startled the dreaming cow, then raced
to the dead tree that stood high on a rise of ground. The bark
of the tree was rough, but Horace shinnied up easily to the
lowest branch and then clambered higher. But the branches
were rotten, and one of them broke. Half-falling, half-slithering,
Horace came down with a bump and rolled over. Rolling over
was so pleasant, he rolled all the way to the bottom of the hill.
When he stood up, covered with dry leaves, his stepfather towered above him.

"Horace," said Dr. Clock mildly, "your mother is looking for
you."

"Oh," said Horace, and he raced ahead of his stepfather to
the stable, where his mother was standing in the doorway, holding baby Gussie.

She said nothing to Horace, but she gave his breeches a soft
slap as he scooted by. "But after all," she whispered to Alexander, "he's only five years old."

"He's got to learn," said Alexander. He thumped his bag
down on the seat of the gig and showed Horace how to help

him hitch up the mare. Mab stood quietly, stretching her neck sideways to chew at the brim of Horace's hat.

When the turnout was ready, Alexander tousled Horace's hair, kissed the baby, kissed his wife, and said, "I'm off to see James."

"Oh, poor James," said Ida, and she pressed her face into Gussie's fat cheek.

Eben was waiting beside the road. Alexander sighed, but he did not complain when his brother-in-law climbed up beside him. Together, they set off down the road to Nashoba to visit Eben's old friend and Alexander's tragic patient, Lt. James Jackson Shaw, shattered by the premature explosion of a shell at the Battle of Five Forks, only eight days before Appomattox.

James had survived, but might it have been better if he had not?

Ida watched them drive away in the direction of Nashoba, their wheels churning up the dust. As she walked into the house holding Horace by the hand and baby Gussie against her shoulder, she wondered how her old friend Isabelle would bear it. And how would Isabelle's mother and father bear it? And what about Ida herself? How would she herself bear the pity of what had happened to Isabelle and her husband, James?

It was not that Ida was timid. She had seen terrible things before. After the Battle of Gettysburg, during her desperate search for her missing husband on the battlefield, she had witnessed an amputation, she had endured the stench of dead horses, she had seen hundreds of badly wounded men, and she had searched among long rows of dead soldiers awaiting burial.

Of course, her second husband, Alexander, had seen even more terrible things. As an army surgeon, Alexander Clock was accustomed to every kind of battle wound, gangrenous and worm-infested, and every kind of dangerous camp fever. He had served in field hospitals in Maryland after the Battle of Antietam, and then as chief surgeon in the Patent Office hospital in Washington. In fact, it had been in the Patent Office that he had first met Ida. She had gone there to look for her missing husband, but she had found her brother Eben instead, dangerously ill with typhoid fever. And it was there that Alexander had fallen in love with her, even as her time came to deliver her baby, the boy who was now bouncing up and down on the sofa in the sitting room.

"Horace?" called Ida's mother. "Are you trying to bring the house down?" Eudocia ran into the sitting room, plopped her grandson down on the sofa, and settled herself beside him. It was time for "Jack and the Beanstalk."

James

With drums and guns, and guns and drums,
The enemy nearly slew ye.
My darling dear, you look so queer,
Oh, Johnny, I hardly knew ye.

—Irish folk song

The mare needed no direction to follow the road to Nashoba. Mab trotted steadily between strawberry fields where people were spreading armfuls of hay. The gig rocked and jiggled as it crossed the bridge over Nashoba Brook. There was no other traffic on the road but a plodding old horse coming the other way, drawing a wagon loaded with a gigantic basket and a strange flabby object of shriveled red and blue. Two men in bowler hats were squeezed together on the seat beside the driver.

Eben nodded as the wagon rattled by. "It's the balloon, I think," he told Alexander.

His brother-in-law had not seen the hot-air balloon of Jack and Jacob Spratt floating over the Milldam that morning. He reached into his pocket and drew out a folded paper. "Perhaps," he said, "you should read this."

Eben had to hold the paper before his eyes with both hands to keep it still. It was Alexander's dry medical assessment, written neatly, like an official report:

THE CASE OF 2ND LT. JAMES JACKSON SHAW, 32ND
MASS. VOL., WOUNDED BY AN EXPLODING SHELL AT
FIVE FORKS, VIRGINIA, APRIL 1, 1865

The wound to the patient's face has resulted in a complete loss of the bony and cartilaginous support of the nose. The tip of the nose has been drawn up and back until the nostrils and columella are so distorted that instead of looking downward the interior nares look directly forward, giving a most dreadful appearance. The shattering of the patient's jaw and the destruction of his tongue have resulted in the loss of articulate speech.

Immediately after Lieutenant Shaw was carried to a hospital tent on the field, both arms were amputated at the wrist. Hooked prosthetic devices were later supplied in Philadelphia.

The extensive wound to the face includes the loss of sight in the left eye. The patient's mental condition is deeply distressing.

Eben handed the note back without a word.

Lieutenant Shaw and his wife, Isabelle, had come home to Nashoba at last, to live in the house of Isabelle's parents, the Reverend Josiah Gideon and his wife, Julia.

The Gideon house stood on a corner, its barn and outbuildings facing the Acton Turnpike. The front door of the house looked across Quarry Pond Road to the burying ground, and across the green to Nashoba's parish church, where the Reverend Horatio

Biddle held sway. Within sight of the house stood the building that was the bailiwick of the Reverend Josiah Gideon himself, a large structure with many windows and a good-size barn. It had once been known to the people of Nashoba as the workhouse, but under the directorship of Josiah Gideon, it was now the Nashoba Home Farm.

The most remarkable feature of this small country town was not a building, but a tree. At the bottom of the sloping burying ground grew a venerable chestnut tree, massive in diameter and lofty in height. It was the pride of Nashoba, famous far and wide as the Nashoba Chestnut. Now in late May, its myriad new leaves trembled in the light breeze as Josiah ducked under the lower limbs and climbed over the stone wall.

He was taking a shortcut from the church after an ugly confrontation with his neighbor, Reverend Biddle. As Josiah crossed the road, his head was still teeming with powerful argument, all the crushing things he might have said. But when he saw the doctor's gig at the gate, his anger dropped away, leaving only the accustomed pang.

The dining room of Josiah's house had been turned over to his wounded son-in-law. The table and the clutter of dining room chairs had been pushed aside to make room for James's upholstered chair, his bed, washstand, and bookshelf, and also for the chair on which Isabelle sat to attend to his needs, which were many and grievous.

James did not look up when Josiah entered the room, but his wife smiled at him and Dr. Clock stood up and shook hands. Isabelle merely glanced up at her father as she tried to slip a spoon into James's mouth. James turned his head away.

Then Josiah was surprised to find another visitor in the room. The young man introduced himself as Eben Flint. "James was my friend before the war," said Eben, "and I think you know my mother, Eudocia."

Josiah tried to sound heartily cordial. "Eudocia Flint, of course."

Isabelle put down her spoon and spoke to Dr. Clock. "I was so sorry to miss your wedding. Your wife was my friend in school."

"Yes," he said, "Ida was sorry, too." It was a painful subject. Everyone in the room knew why Isabelle had missed the wedding. She had been with James, following him from one hospital to another while army surgeons did all they could for him.

There was an awkward silence. Eben could not look at Isabelle, and he did not know whether it would be kinder to look straight into James's face as he would with any normal friend or look away.

But Isabelle's mother spoke to Eben gently. "Your little nephew must be a big boy now." Then Julia turned to Alexander. "And I hear he has a baby sister." Quietly, she added, "I'm so sorry about the loss of your first little one."

It was apparent to Alexander that her sympathy was genuine, and he was touched and grateful. But the tension in the room was unbearable. It could not be good for James. Alexander caught Eben's eye and stood up, promising to return before long.

Eben looked straight into James's face and said, "So will I."

Josiah and Julia accompanied their two visitors to the door, but it was a silent departure. What, after all, was there to say?

Alone with James, Isabelle dipped the spoon once again in the bowl and said calmly, "Remember, James? These peaches are from the summer when you first came calling. Remember how you stoked the stove?" Lifting the spoon, she said again, "They came out very well."

But once again, James turned his head away.

If it were only that he were half-blind, he could have borne it lightly. Or if he were half-blind and had but one arm how easy it would have been to be a man like other men. Yes, even if he were half-blind and both hands were missing, he could have borne it somehow. But to be half-blind and armless, with a face that was a mask of horror—it was more than he could bear.

James closed his single eye and prayed. Let them stop breaking their hearts over me. Let them give up trying to help me. Let Isabelle stop wasting her life to care for me. Please God, let me go.

A Sad
Connecting Cord

There was another crisis at home. As Mab whirled around the corner into the yard, hungry for the oats in her stall, Ida came running out to meet them, tearing off her apron and calling, "It's Horace—he's gone again."

At once, they scattered to look, and Eben soon found his small nephew on the roof of the henhouse.

Horace was stuck there, afraid to come down. He had gone up the back of the shed roof like Jack climbing the bean stalk, shifted his boots to the windowsill, reached up to the ringbolt for the clothesline, grasped the edge of the roof, thrown one leg over, and scrambled up easily. At the top of the roof, he had perched in triumph, king of the henhouse, lord of the bean stalk. But getting down was another matter. The slope of the roof was steep, the ground far away. And the peevish turkey was flapping across the hen yard to gobble at him, wagging its red wattles and spreading its tail, eager to nip poor Horace. Then Horace remembered the roar of the giant in his grandmother's story—"Fe-fi-fo-fum"—and he began to cry.

When Eben found him, Horace was clinging forlornly to the stovepipe. "Hang on, Horace," said Eben, "I'll get a ladder."

But when he was safely deposited on the ground, Horace cheered up right away. It was clear that he had not learned a thing. Alexander scolded him anyway, his mother hugged him, and his grandmother carried him into the kitchen, where gingerbread was fresh and hot. Eben went to the stable to rub down Mab's steaming sides, and then he walked slowly into the house and climbed the stairs.

Left alone with Alexander, Ida said, "How is James?" When he only shook his head, she said nothing more.

But for the rest of the day there was a sense that the two houses were joined. Their comfortable house in Concord was attached to that other house in Nashoba. In actual miles, the two houses were not far apart, and now they were linked by a sad connecting cord. Eben could feel it thrumming in the walls, trying to tug the house out of the ground and drag it westward. The illusion was strong. This familiar homestead set among lilacs and a neglected apple orchard, this noisy house echoing with the banging of his mother's piano and the wheezing of her reed organ and the sentimental singing of his sister Sallie— "Last night the nightingale woke me"—and the cries of baby Augusta and the shrill games of Eben's brother, Josh, and his sister Alice and his nephew, Horace, this house that was quiet at the same time with Ida's reading and Alexander's writing and Eben's thinking, was now linked by a cord of sympathy that stretched taut above the orchard and Nashoba Brook and the town line and the chestnut tree to the house on Quarry Pond Road, where James Jackson Shaw sat with bowed head, bereft among the dining room chairs.

And therefore it was strange that Eben's dream that night was not a nightmare vision of the ravaged face of James, with his mutilated arms and single suffering eye; it was a dream about a woman whose face was vague, her identity unsure. Was it Ella Viles whose nightdress he was tearing off, Ella's breasts he was caressing?

Eben sat up in a sweat. Awake, he knew it had not been Ella who had so sweetly returned his ardor in his dream. No, no, it had not been Ella Viles.

NOW

The Necessity
for Steeples

From this window I can compare the written with the preached word: within is weeping, and wailing, and gnashing of teeth; without, grain fields and grasshoppers, which give those the lie direct.

—Henry Thoreau, *Journal,*
July 8, 1838

Homer's Fame

A strange mania had gripped the readers of the nation. Homer Kelly's little monograph, *Hen and Chicks,* was the talk of cocktail parties. Glitzy bars buzzed with Homer's name. It did not seem to matter that few people had read past the first obscure pages, because everyone fully intended to pick up the book any minute now.

Success went to Homer's head. But that was all right, decided Mary. For the last year, the poor man had felt the day of his retirement looming closer and closer, and it was an added insult that her own star kept rising at the same time. Whenever the phone rang, Homer would jump to answer it, only to say glumly, "She's right here," and hand it over. In fact, things had become so sticky, Mary had begun to keep her small triumphs to herself.

Now things were different. Homer was in demand every-where. The chairman of Harvard's Committee on Academic Honors wanted to speak to him. And would Professor Kelly address the Academy of Arts and Sciences? Would he accept a Lifetime Achievement Award from the Modern Language Association?

So now it was Mary's turn to hand over the phone with a dry remark—"It's NPR," or "It's the *New York Review of Books.*"

"The trouble is," said Homer after agreeing to be filmed while puttering around his delightful riverside residence or sitting at his keyboard composing another chapter of a thrilling new work to be called *Steeplechase,* "there's no time left to write the damn book."

So when his editor called again at dawn, it was the last straw. A joyful shout came over the phone, "*Sex,* I forgot about *sex.*"

"Well, that's too bad," said Homer, sitting up in bed and rubbing his ear. "I never forget it for a single moment."

"I mean in those churches of yours," gabbled Luther. "The preacher eloping with the choirmistress, fornication in the cloister, copulation in the crypt."

"There ain't no cloisters in these here churches," growled Homer. "Nor no crypts, neither."

"Well, I don't care where it happened, but it must have happened somewhere. Fornication any old place on the sacred premises, okay? Screwing in the steeple? Hey, that's pretty good. Readers, they'll eat it up, and you got another bestseller."

"I can't believe it," said Homer, dumping sugar in his breakfast coffee. "Luther's a distinguished editor at a dignified old university press. What's gotten into him?"

"He wants to make another killing—that's what's gotten into him. But you know what, Homer? He may be right."

"Right!" Homer was scandalized. "The preacher and the choirmistress? Screwing in the steeple?"

"Well, no, probably nothing as sensational as that. But I'll bet those pious old church histories don't always tell the whole truth." Mary clattered the breakfast dishes into the sink. "Come on, let's get away from the phone and chase a few steeples. I'll bet all the churches around here have skeletons of some kind or other in their closets."

"Good, where shall we start?"

"Right here in Concord. Why not? We can begin with the First Parish. Then we could talk to the Trinitarians. And who else? The rabbi of Temple Emanuel?"

"Temple Emanuel? No, no, Mary dear, think about it. The temple isn't exactly a hatchling from a Protestant chicken yard."

"Of course not. Moses and Jeremiah sat on that egg. And anyway, temples don't have steeples."

"Right," said Homer. "We gotta have steeples."

1868

Eternal Remembrances

*Like a spirit land of shadows
They in silence on me gaze
And I feel my heart is beating
With the pulse of other days;
And I ask what great magician
Conjured forms like these afar?
Echo answers, 'tis the sunshine,
By its alchemist Daguerre.*

—Caleb Lyon, 1850

"Welcome, Ladies and Gents!"

Mrs. Ida Clock   Dr. Alexander Clock

The brothers Spratt looked so much alike, people couldn't tell Jake from Jack. But their talents were different.

"My Jackie," their mother boasted, "he's the artistic one. Jackie can paint you a bouquet so natural, you could pick the posies. His brother, he's just the opposite. Jakie's always a-tinkering."

Thus it was Jack Spratt who set up the elegant chamber for portrait photography in their horse-drawn mobile studio. And it was Jack who furnished it with a thronelike chair, a balustrade, a hollow column, a carpet-covered table, and a velvet curtain with an imposing tassel.

But it was Jake who understood the wet-plate process and knew how to turn out any number of albumen prints from a single glass negative.

Then it was Jack's turn again. It was his clever scissors that snipped out the images, his nimble fingers that mounted them on pretty pieces of cardboard, and his high-flown eloquence that fluttered down from the basket of the balloon:

Jack and Jacob Spratt

Aerial and Portrait Photographers
Cartes de Visite, cabinet photographs
Men, women, children and babes
Mortuarie images a specialty

On the Saturday in May when the mobile studio of the Spratt brothers pulled up on the green between Concord's Middlesex Hotel and the courthouse, there were no mortuary requirements, although Jack and Jake had made tender images of many a dead baby—Jack arranging the little hands sweetly on the infant's breast, Jake comforting the weeping mother.

This morning, they were not surprised to find customers already waiting. The Spratt brothers were accustomed to success. "All kindsa people want their pitchers taken, Jack," said Jake.

"Only natural, Jake," said Jack. "In this cruel world, who knows when a person might take sick and die without no eternal remembrance of their physiognomy while blood still pulsed in their veins?"

Jake jumped down and unhitched the team while Jack shifted the noble appointments into place and pulled back the shade over the skylight. Then, poking his head through the curtains, he lifted his hat. "Welcome, ladies and gents! Who's first?"

It was a small boy. The boy's mother kept an anxious eye on him as Jack helped him up into the wagon. But Horace was on his best behavior. Delighted to have his picture taken, he stood smartly erect and smiled into the camera.

Ida was next. She handed the baby to her mother, climbed into the wagon, and sat down beside the carpet-covered table.

Ida's husband, Alexander, came running up from the North

Road to take his turn. He was carrying his doctor's bag because
he had been attending the deathbed of the Widow Plankton. It
was the widow's fourth deathbed, and doubtless there would be
a fifth. As Ida stepped down and took the baby from her
mother, Alexander jumped up into the wagon.

In the artistic judgment of the photographer, this client had a
noble profile. "Sir," said Jack, "I recommend you look to the
side."

Alexander obeyed, waited for the flash of light, and then
jumped down from the wagon. Once again, the man in the
bowler hat stuck out his head. "All right, folks, who desires to
be next?"

Eudocia had disappeared with Alice to go shopping on the
Milldam. "Your turn, Eben," said Alexander. "Go ahead. It
doesn't hurt a bit."

Eben had been waiting to take everybody home. "My turn?"
he said. "Well, I don't know."

Jack Spratt looked at Eben, his eyebrows high, his face a question mark. "Sir, would you be pleased to have your likeness
taken?"

It was easier to do it than not, so Eben's face, too, was recorded
for eternity.

A Philosophical
Dispute

The Spratt brothers had come to Concord at a good time, because it was the day of the cattle fair. This huge event occupied acres of ground behind the depot on the other side of the railroad tracks, but Concord center was also teeming with visitors. Carriages bustled up and down the Milldam as interested parties arrived from all the surrounding towns.

Some of them had urgent transactions to conduct at the fair, but most were drawn by the general air of excitement. Alert to the opportunity, shopkeepers along the Milldam had stocked their shelves with fancy goods. Bonnets in one shopwindow were decked with ribbons and flowers, and in front of the greengrocer lay baskets of asparagus. At one corner of the green, the Middlesex Hotel was doing a land-office business in West Indian rum, brandy, gin, and cider, and the town was awash in oysters fresh from the train.

There was a new war memorial in the center of the green, an obelisk adorned with bronze tablets. One of the tablets listed the names of the Concord men who had never come back, including the name of Ida's first husband, Seth Morgan. The other tablet was a tribute:

THE TOWN OF CONCORD

BUILDS THIS MONUMENT

IN HONOR OF

THE BRAVE MEN

WHOSE NAMES IT BEARS:

AND RECORDS WITH GRATEFUL PRIDE

THAT THEY FOUND HERE

A BIRTHPLACE, HOME OR GRAVE.

Eben leaned against the pedestal. He was waiting for the rest of his family to be photographed, but it looked to be a long wait. By the time his mother and little sisters came back from the Milldam, a line of other customers had collected in front of the mobile studio of the brothers Spratt.

"Oh, dear," said Eudocia, "we shouldn't have gone shopping." They took their places at the end of the line, Sallie in a new bonnet, Alice in a new pinafore. Through the open windows of the Middlesex Hotel came the sound of drunken guffaws, and on the hotel porch a knot of men in top hats stood in a cloud of tobacco smoke. Eben watched the knot dissolve and trickle across the road. They were like iron filings drawn by the magnet of the painted sign advertising the photographic services of Jack and Jacob Spratt.

With baby Gussie whimpering on her shoulder, Eben's sister Ida was trying to keep track of Horace, but he kept darting away, skipping up and down the line, smiling up at the men in stovepipe hats. One of them handed him a sticky black gumdrop. "Here, boy, want a nigger baby?"

"No, no, Horace," called Ida, running up to take his hand. But Horace was nearly bursting with the excitement of the crowded green, the men with candy in their pockets, the horses, the carriages, the noise, the fat boy playing a tin whistle. When Ida pulled him away, his excitement boiled over and he began to bawl. Inspired by his example, Gussie bawled, too.

"Here," said Eben, "let me take him." Swiftly, he picked up Horace, tossed him up on his shoulders, and bore him away to the place in front of the courthouse where he had left Mab and the spring wagon. Somehow, the entire family had crowded into the buggy—Eben driving, Sallie with Alice on her lap, Eudocia with Horace, and Ida holding the baby. Now Mab was waiting sleepily with her head down beside the curb, but she perked up when she saw Horace.

"Look, Horace," said Eben, lifting his nephew up on the front seat, "you can see everything better from here."

Uncle Eben was right. Horace bounced on the high seat and looked around happily at the waiting crowd, the green trees, the barking dog, the cat slinking across the street, the photographer poking his head out of his wagon, the baker's cart.

And there was excitement here, too. As Uncle Eben climbed up to sit beside him, they heard an explosion of cursing on the road, a squawking of chickens, a stamping of horses. It was a near collision. A dray loaded with hen coops was blocking the way of a carriage occupied by two gentlemen and three ladies. Chickens screeched and feathers flew, but the driver of the carriage refused to budge. The sulky drayman had to back his team out of the way to permit the two carriage horses to step smartly into the empty space beside Eben's wagon.

At once, Eben was aware of the presence of Isabelle Shaw.

She was wedged in the back of the carriage between her mother and Mrs. Biddle. In front sat Isabelle's father, Josiah Gideon, and the Reverend Horatio Biddle. The two men were in heated argument. Behind them, the women sat shocked and silent. Both disputants were clergymen, but the peace of God was not in evidence. Eben said a polite good morning and nodded at the ladies, but only Isabelle's mother gave him a wan smile. When the three women began gathering their skirts to descend, he jumped down to help, but Isabelle was too quick for him. Before he could take her hand, she was standing in the road, assisting Mrs. Biddle. Isabelle's mother took Eben's hand gratefully, but the two men on the forward seats made no move to step down. They were still in hot dispute.

Isabelle looked around as though she had forgotten why they had come. Julia took her arm and together they walked across the green toward the studio of the photographers. Mrs. Biddle followed, tugging off her gloves and popping up her parasol, her lips compressed.

Disappointed, Eben climbed back on the wagon, pretending not to hear the tempest of dialectic beside him, but Horace stared openmouthed. The faces of the two men were red with anger, their voices passionate and loud. Yet the content of their disagreement was purely philosophical. It was a classic argument, like the debates of Eben's student days. Listening, keeping his eyes on Mab's cocked ears, he soon had a title for this one—"Query: whether the truths of science and the revelations of religion be not fundamentally opposed."

Debater Josiah had taken the negative: No, they were not opposed, and only at its peril might religion ignore the great new truths of science.

Reverend Horatio argued vehemently for the positive. The so-called truths of the new science were not true at all, but false. They were undermining the faith of the fathers, spreading doubt and confusion in the hearts of Christian believers.

"Sir," said Josiah, "you must have heard of Mr. Darwin's great book?"

"Sir," replied Horatio, "you must have read Professor Agassiz's reply?"

It was a standoff. Eben kept his eyes fixed on the men lounging on the steps of the courthouse, but he listened with all his might. Horace gaped and stared. Even Mab flicked her ears, as if she were listening, too.

"Don't Tell!"

Isabelle and James Shaw, 1864   Isabelle Shaw, 1868

Next?" said the photographer in the bowler hat. This time, it was Jake Spratt, taking over from his exhausted brother, but the customers were not aware of the difference, because Jake was the spitting image of Jack.

There were only a few customers left by the time the party from Nashoba took its place in line. Isabelle found herself just behind Ella Viles.

Ella had frizzed her hair with curlpapers, and she looked fetching in a ribbon bow. At once, she leaned close to Isabelle and murmured, "My likeness is for Eben."

Isabelle was startled. "You mean Eben Flint?"

"Of course," whispered Ella. "We're promised." Slyly, she rolled her eyes sideways to the place where Eben and his small nephew waited beside the wagon in which Isabelle's father and Mr. Biddle were still sitting stiffly upright.

"Promised? You are?" In spite of herself, Isabelle could not hide her dismay. Not for herself, of course, but for Eben—that he should settle for a girl like Ella Viles.

"It's a secret," whispered Ella. "Promise you won't tell."

Isabelle mumbled something, but she was grateful when her old friend Ida came hurrying up to embrace her just as Jake Spratt poked his head out of the curtain and said, "Which of you ladies is next?"

Eudocia Flint was next, then Alice and Sallie. Next in line was Isabelle's mother, Julia Gideon. Julia settled herself dreamily beside the carpeted table, remembering the itinerant photographer who had come to Nashoba in the summer of '64, just before her new son-in-law had left to join his regiment. The new husband and wife had been taken together, James seated and Isabelle standing beside him with her hand on his shoulder. Julia had seen other photographs like it—anxious wives touching, clasping, leaning close to husbands who were about to endure the dangers of the battlefield.

James had endured them and survived, and now he was home again, but the brothers Spratt would not be taking his picture. Not this day, nor any other. Only his wife would be recorded for all future time, for Jack Spratt's "eternity"—Isabelle alone.

"All done, Jack," said Jake, looking out at the empty green.

"Still early, Jake," said Jack.

"Three plates left," said Jake.

"Let's use 'em up," said Jack.

So they sat for each other—Jack looking one way, Jake the other. The last plate recorded a pretty view of the town green, and then, their day's work done, they closed up shop.

NOW

The First Steeple

> *Concord*
> *30 April 1865*
>
> *Dear Sir,*
> *I notify you of my*
> *wish to become a*
> *member of the First*
> *Parish.*
>
> *Respectfully*
> *R. W. Emerson*

Skeleton in the Closet

First Parish, Concord

Heads together, Homer and Mary bent over the old photograph of Concord's Monument Square. Rising tall and pale in the foreground stood the Civil War memorial obelisk. In the middle distance, large and foursquare, was the Middlesex Hotel with horses and buggies drawn up in front of the porch. They could just make out the steeple of the First Parish Church high over the trees beyond the hotel.

"Picture taken in 1868," murmured Homer.

"Photographs are so haunting," said Mary. "Monument Square must have looked just like this when my great-great-grandmother Ida was alive, and my great-grandfather must have been a small boy in 1868."

"And Ida's brother Eben—remember Eben Flint? He would

have been twenty-one in 1868. But her husband Seth was dead by then."

"Oh, poor misunderstood Seth. Was Ida married again by 1868? Yes, I think she was. So her second husband, the doctor, he would have seen it like this. In 1868, Alexander must have been living with Ida in the house on Barrett's Mill Road." Mary stroked the photograph. "If only we could walk into the picture and see what it looked like then, the house I grew up in." Mary sighed with longing. "Oh, if only the picture would open up and let us in."

"I know," said Homer. "It's too bad. But we can still walk into the church." He tapped the dim bell tower in the picture. "It's our first steeple. The photograph won't open up, but maybe the church archivist will. Maybe he'll tell us something scandalous about the history of the First Parish, so that I can satisfy the shameless curiosity of my editor. Luther keeps calling up, demanding skeletons in the closet, vice and corruption, screwing in the—"

"Oh, never mind what went on in the steeple." Mary laughed. "Homer, what on earth has happened to Luther Stokes? How could such a distinguished doctor of philosophy and celebrated director of a university press turn into a Peeping Tom?"

Homer shrugged. "Let's hope this chap Henry Whipple knows about a few tasty scandals."

"Oh, Homer, I doubt it. A scandal in Concord? In this upright old town? Surely none of those august old clergymen had skeletons in their closets. Nothing but old boots and dusty umbrellas."

Homer met Henry Whipple at the side door of the church, but at once Henry steered him elsewhere. "My house is right next door," he said, heading for the road. "We'll talk in my study."

In his study, thought Homer. On the way, struggling to keep up, he wondered eagerly about the nature of Henry's study. Homer was a connoisseur of other people's working arrangements. How, for instance, did they keep their pens and pencils, and where did they put their stamps? Did they stick up notes around their computer monitors about passwords and user IDs and reminders to pick up their pants at the cleaner's? And, above all, how did they control their teeming collections of pamphlets and folders, books and notebooks, miscellaneous pieces of paper, unanswered letters, and all the ragtag strokes of genius scribbled down on the backs of envelopes? What about their dictionaries? And by the way, what other reference books did they keep on hand to be snatched up at a moment's notice?

As it turned out, Henry Whipple's arrangements were charming. He had built himself a nest around his keyboard. Small high-piled tables were gathered in close to take the overflow. A comfy sweater hung over the back of a chair to ward off a chill, and a whirly fan stood beside the printer in case of a heat wave. All that was missing in Henry's nest was a lining of downy feathers.

And to Homer's delight, Henry was ready at once to reveal a blot on the escutcheon of Concord's old First Parish Church. "How about a hanging sermon?" he said. "Will that do?"

"A hanging sermon?" said Homer joyfully. "No kidding?"

"No indeed." Henry sat back and said smugly, "The Reverend Dr. Ripley preached a hanging sermon in 1799."

"Ezra Ripley? Pious old Dr. Ripley?" Homer's eyes bulged. "But that's impossible. You don't mean the same dear old Ezra Ripley who was pastor of the First Parish for years and years?"

"Sixty years, that's right. I do indeed." Then Henry frowned. "But I don't know as I'd call him 'dear.' He was a pretty authoritarian old—" Stopping himself, Henry reached for a book and flipped it open.

Homer was merciless. "Pretty authoritarian old what?"

"Never mind," said Henry, busily turning pages. "Back to the hanging sermon. You know, Homer, it wasn't anything out of the ordinary for the time." Then Henry slammed the book shut and looked at Homer fiercely. "First, you've got to picture the congregation in the old church, all the pews packed with people eager to witness a hanging, and the unhappy victim sitting smack in front of the pulpit while the pastor scolded him for his criminal ways. Okay, Homer, you get the picture?" Henry opened the book again. "Here's what Ripley said to poor old Samuel Smith. 'Your life for thirty years past has been a predatory warfare against society and individual families and persons.'"

"Samuel Smith was the—ah—hangee?"

"Right," said Henry, and he went on to describe the scene on Gallows Hill, with Smith pleading for his life, then dancing a fandango in the air with the rope around his neck and women fainting and lying on the ground with their fair legs exposed. "Well, I suppose it was their legs," said Henry. "In George W. Hosmer's memoir, the word *fair* is followed by four asterisks."

"Hmmm," said Homer, looking at the ceiling. "What else could they have exposed that had only four letters?"

"Nothing in George Hosmer's vocabulary," said the archivist firmly, and he went on to tell Homer about Parson Ripley's distress over the drunkenness and disorder in the town and his passionate reaction to the schism in his congregation. "He fought it tooth and nail," said Henry, shaking his head in awe. "He walked right into a gathering of dissenters and preached a sermon, so the poor people had to sit there and listen. But he couldn't prevent them from formally withdrawing from the congregation. What they wanted, they said, was 'a more active spiritual life.' Well, I guess they were objecting to the appearance of the Unitarian heresy in Dr. Ripley's church. So away they went, and set up a church of their own."

Homer nodded wisely. "Yes, of course. The Trinitarian Congregational Church on Walden Street. It's one of my chicks."

"What do you think, Mary darling?" said Homer, climbing into bed beside her. "Is it scandal enough for my editor? Will Luther be satisfied with a nasty schism in the church, Trinitarians waltzing off, two churches ringing their Sabbath bells in competition, and a hanging sermon?"

"I don't know, Homer. It isn't exactly sex in the steeple."

"Well then, I could add a few pages about sex on Fairhaven Bay," said Homer, drawing her close.

"I'm afraid it doesn't exactly fit your subject. I mean, you couldn't call it a skeleton in the closet of the First Parish Church. And how on earth would you itemize it in the index?"

"Under 'Sex, contemporary,'" said Homer. "Luther would like it, I'll bet."

Homer's sleep was often entertained by lurid visions. Tonight, he dreamed about Luther's metaphorical skeleton in the closet. This skeleton, however, was not a metaphor, but a tidy collection of ribs and miscellaneous other bones lying right there beside him, nudging Mary to the edge of the bed. While he stared at it in disbelief, the skeleton reared up on one bony elbow and looked back at him with a sparkle in the hollow socket of its eye.

1868

The Enormous Tree

Crossed from the top of Annursnack to the top of Strawberry Hill. . . . Measured the great chestnut. . . . It branches first at nine feet from the ground, with great furrows in the bark.

—Henry Thoreau, *Journal,*
August 15, 1854

Josiah

The Reverend Josiah Gideon

Josiah walked home from the church, hardly able to contain his anger. Horatio Biddle had aimed a tirade like a blast from a cannon straight at the head of Josiah Gideon as he sat alone in the family pew. Passages from the Bible had been hurled at him like mortar shells, as though the Book of Genesis were the sole property of Horatio Biddle, as though Josiah had trampled it underfoot and desecrated the evening and the morning, the beasts of the earth, and the fowl of the air. Then Horatio Biddle had raised a sanctimonious hand and vowed never to profane the house of God with the name of the British naturalist who had replaced their great ancestors Adam and Eve with ludicrous hairy beasts. And then he had waxed poetic, telling again the fable about the wood of the tree in the Garden of Eden that had become the cross of Christ.

Straight downhill through the burial ground strode Josiah, his long legs carrying him at high speed past the ancient headstones of the first settlers of Nashoba.

The tree in the garden and the cross of Christ! Oh, yes, it was a pretty story, but it belonged to Josiah Gideon as rightfully as it did to Horatio Biddle. And there was another legendary tree, one of which Horatio was entirely unaware.

Josiah paused in his downhill plunge and looked up at the chestnut tree beside the stone wall. It was a gigantic tree, spreading its green crown all the way across the Acton Road to drop its cool shade on his own doorstep. Surely the tree had towered over the graves of the first settlers of Nashoba, and over the memorial stones of the sad generation that followed, when whole families had been swept away by scarlet fever and the bloody flux.

But to Josiah, it had become much more than a splendid survivor from centuries past. He now thought of it as Mr. Darwin's great "Tree of Life." He knew the passage by heart and he mumbled it now as he climbed over the wall:

> As buds give rise by growth to fresh buds, and these, if vigorous, branch out and overtop on all sides many a feebler branch, so by generation I believe it has been with the great Tree of Life, which fills with its dead and broken branches the crust of the earth, and covers the surface with its ever-branching and beautiful ramifications.

If ever a living tree could be said to have "ever-branching and beautiful ramifications," it was the chestnut tree in the Nashoba burial ground. Josiah's anger seized on the tree as a rallying center for all his mental forces.

But as he vaulted the stone wall, he saw the doctor's horse browsing on the grass beside the gate. Once again, he tried to clear his mind of its feverish excitement, because within that house, where at this moment a curtain was blowing out of a bedroom window and the shadow of the chestnut tree was moving over the clapboards, there could be only one thought. Before it, all others fell away. Josiah's daughter, Isabelle, flinging open the door to welcome him, was an embodiment of the thought, the doctor spoke it aloud in quiet truths, and James was the thought itself.

Once again, Eben Flint had come with the doctor. Eben nodded at Josiah, then looked back at James. Isabelle and Julia stood watching, too, as James tried to undo the buckles of the prosthetic hook on his left arm with the hook on his right. He failed, and failed again, and at last the hook clattered to the floor.

"Good," murmured Alexander. He took the stump in his hand and inspected the raw chafing. "I'll bring something next time. I've got an ointment that's first-rate."

Eben said quickly, "I think I could make a better fit than that."

James made a sound in his throat. He was not interested in a better fit and he cared little for an ointment to soothe the chafing. He could not say what he wanted in words. He could only gaze at the doctor with his one suffering eye.

Alexander did not need words. In a field hospital after Antietam, he had seen the same look on the face of a maimed lieutenant from Mississippi. In everything but words, James was pleading, Help me out of this sorrow. Of course, Dr. Clock pretended not to understand. He closed his bag and said a serene good-bye. Eben followed him out of the room, and so did Isabelle and Josiah.

In the hall, Eben took his hat from the table and said to Josiah, "You see, sir, I could make a sort of padded contraption that might be more comfortable for James. I'll see what I can do."

Eben could not look at Isabelle, but when Josiah thanked him, so did she.

For the rest of the day, the house was quiet. Isabelle took down a book from the Dickens shelf, but when she showed it to James, he shook his head and pointed a hook at another. "You mean this one?" said Isabelle. He nodded, and she plucked it out. Sitting down beside him, settling herself comfortably among the chair cushions, Isabelle began to read *A Tale of Two Cities: "It was the best of times, it was the worst of times."*

James bowed his head and listened.

Upstairs, Josiah was reading, too. He had set up an office under the eaves of the spare room and arranged on the desk his lexicon, his quill pens, his penknife, his household ledger, and the account books for the charitable institutions that were in his care. Here also was the Bible that had belonged to his father and grandfather before him. Its covers were cracked and its pages limp from a thousand turnings—his father's hand seeking one of Paul's Epistles, his grandfather turning to the Book of Revelation.

Josiah picked up the heavy book and opened it to the beginning. He had not looked at Genesis since his days in seminary. Now he read the first three chapters from the beginning all the way to the verse about the angel whose flaming sword drove Adam away from the tree of life.

The story was a wonder. Josiah sank back in his chair and read the beautiful verses over and over, until, to his surprise, he saw that Adam's tree was beginning to merge with that other tree, the one that teemed with birds and monkeys, lions and tigers. A chimpanzee scrambled past him and a bird of paradise flew so close that its feathers brushed his face, and a kindly baboon reached out its hand.

"Josiah?" His wife was touching his shoulder, and he woke with a start. Julia stood beside him in her nightdress. Josiah lighted a candle, and their shadows followed them across the hall. In the bedroom, he blew out the candle, put his arm around his wife and led her to the window. In a moment, their eyes adjusted to the darkness. Julia drew the curtain aside, and at once they could see the stars, although half the sky was blotted out by the dark shape of the enormous tree across the road.

Charles Darwin had said nothing about the stars.

The Emperor's Birds

Ella Viles

The photographs had come. Jake Spratt had developed the plates and printed the images, and Jack had mounted them on cards and dispatched them in brown paper packets.

All over Concord and Nashoba, the subjects of the pictures tore off the brown paper and extracted the contents. Some of the subjects were disappointed and threw their images in the stove; others were pleased and ordered more.

Ella Viles was delighted with her set of six cartes de visite. At once, she urged her mother to pay a call on Eudocia Flint.

Her mother objected. "Eudocia and I never call. She belongs to the Charitable Society, and that set of women is altogether too freethinking, in my opinion. I prefer the ladies of the Eastern Star."

But Ella had her way. And therefore mother and daughter set out on a Wednesday morning in their pretty Jenny Lind, Mrs. Viles shading her complexion with a parasol, Ella flourishing a dainty whip.

Eudocia was astonished to see them at the door. "Well, my goodness, come in," she said, sweeping off her apron. Turning quickly to the little boy beside her, she said, "Horace dear, we'll read your story later." But the boy clung unhappily to his grandmother's skirt as the two elegant ladies stepped inside.

Their visit was a failure because Eben was not at home. Disappointed, Ella folded her hands in her lap and listened to her mother's probing gossip: "Eudocia, have you heard about that poor young man in Nashoba, the one with the horrible wounds who is married to Ella's friend Isabelle?"

"No," lied Eudocia stoutly, "I have not." Horace climbed into her lap and sucked his thumb. Conversation languished. Eudocia did not offer tea.

Ruffled, Ella and her mother rose to go. But at the door, Ella thrust a packet into Eudocia's hand. "Eben asked for my likeness," she said, simpering. "Tell him I demand one of his in return."

"I'll tell him," said Eudocia crisply.

With relief, she watched the pretty buggy dip and rock as Ella and Mrs. Viles climbed in. When the little cob trotted away with one of Eudocia's prize tulips dangling from its mouth, she closed the door smartly and put her arm around her grandson. "Come on, Horace dear," she said, plumping him down on the sofa in the sitting room, "it's time for your story."

It was a brand-new book of fairy tales. Today's story was "The Emperor's Nightingale." When Eben came home, he tossed his hat on a chair, sat down beside Horace, and listened, too.

"The artificial bird," read Eudocia, *"was covered with diamonds, rubies, and sapphires. As soon as its key was wound, it could sing and move its tail up and down. But the plain little brown bird sang to the emperor about the quiet churchyard where the white roses grow, where the elder tree wafts its perfume on the breeze."*

It was the end of the story. "Read it again!" said Horace.

But Eudocia closed the book, reached for the packet left by Ella Viles, and handed it to Eben. "This is for you. Two ladies brought it this morning. Delivered by hand."

"For me?" Puzzled, Eben opened the packet and found the photograph of Ella Viles.

"She demands one of yours in return," said Eudocia dryly.

"She does?" Eben stared at Ella's high-piled curls, then put the picture in the pocket of his coat, reflecting on the emperor's two birds and on the nature of two women of his acquaintance. Which was the twittering clockwork bird and which the nightingale?

The Home Farm

The steeple of Nashoba's parish church was imposing, but it was not a white needle pointing at the sky. It was a domed tower with a bell chamber and a clock.

Behind the church on the road to Acton stood the parsonage of the Reverend Horatio Biddle. From the front door, Horatio and his wife, Ingeborg, could look down the whole length of the burial ground to the place where the chestnut tree marked the edge of the graveyard. Across Quarry Pond Road, hidden by the gigantic canopy of leaves, was the home of Horatio's fractious parishioner Josiah Gideon. In front of the church stretched the rough grass of the town green, and beyond the green stood another building painful to the sight of Horatio Biddle. Josiah Gideon called it the Nashoba Home Farm, which

was only his fancy name for the old Nashoba poorhouse, so long
a depository for bastard and orphaned children, the aged and in-
firm, the feebleminded and insane.

The Nashoba Home Farm was not the only almshouse su-
pervised by Josiah Gideon. He had been appointed by the Massachusetts State Board of Charities to inspect all the almshouses
in Middlesex County. Therefore, he spent three days a week
touring the countryside, interviewing caretakers, examining in-
firmaries, laundries, and kitchens, and taking note of provisions
for heat and light, fresh air and exercise, washing and bathing.

As a Christian clergyman, Josiah had been drawn to this
work by observing that the greatest need for human courage
came at the time of greatest weakness—in old age or desperate
poverty. Thank God, things were no longer as inhumane as they
had once been, back in the bad old days when town charges
were auctioned off "at public venue" to the lowest bidder and
exploited for their labor. No longer might their dead bodies be
handed over for dissection to medical schools in order to further "the advancement of medical science." No, things were no
longer as bad as that. Most of the almshouses inspected by Josiah
were run by competent superintendents and matrons. The others aroused his furious pity and relentless nagging.

In Nashoba, Josiah's fiery eye had cowed the overseers of the
poor into financing a model home for the indigent. The result
was a handsome addition to the old workhouse and a new barn
equipped with livestock and outfitted with all the tools and machinery necessary to a thriving agricultural enterprise. There
were horse rakes and plows, a mowing machine, a cultivator, a
mechanical seeder, a spring-tooth harrow, a dozen sap buckets,
and a plentiful supply of hand tools.

Compared to the Boston House of Industry, the entire estab-
lishment was small. But Josiah had vowed that the inmates of
the Home Farm would turn a profit from the wasted fields and
common grazing land belonging to the town. In addition, they
would put the sugar bush to use and cut a swath through the

town forest, a wilderness like some far uncharted corner of the globe.

It had not been easy. The board of selectmen had balked at the expense. Josiah had received a formal letter: "The board would by no means favor an unnecessary expenditure in building ornamental palaces, either for criminals or paupers, nor do they wish even to make such a house attractive to the idle."

Josiah Gideon cared nothing for official letters. At the next meeting of the selectmen, he had ranted and raved, and prevailed.

Dickie Doll

Dickie Doll

S ome of the elderly citizens of Nashoba were slow to learn
of the marvels called for by Josiah Gideon. For them, the
word *workhouse* still meant a fate to be dreaded more than death
itself. "I'd sooner lie down and die in a ditch by the side of the
road," said old Dickie Doll.

But now the ditch yawned for Dickie at last. His home and
hire were gone. Miss Lydia Perkins, the old widow whose hired
man he had been for most of his life, had taken sick and died. Her
property was to go on the auction block—her fields and woods,
her crops, and her house and barn, along with the shed where
Dickie had so long slept and plied his woodworking trade.

Josiah Gideon sought him out. Josiah's disfigured son-in-law,
James Shaw, was beyond any help that he could give, no matter

how eagerly he longed to do something, anything, to help poor James. Therefore, he took comfort in tracking down any misery within his power to ease. He rode out to the remotest edges of the town, knocking on the doors of lonely farms to find addled old grannies, superannuated old gentlemen fading into eccentricity, hungry paupers in neglected shanties, Irish field hands who came and went like Gypsies, and even the half-wild men who lived by gun and snare and rabbit trap in the depths of the town forest.

On the day of the auction, Josiah moved among the sharp dealers who were examining the rolling stock that had belonged to the Widow Perkins, and the housewives interested in her sideboard, bedstead, and mangle, and the local farmers who were there to inspect her dairy cattle. Josiah was looking for Dickie Doll. He found him sitting forlornly among his tools while a man in a seedy stovepipe hat dumped a box of Dickie's chisels on the ground and spat and drawled, "These here for sale?"

"Can't say as I care," said Dickie.

"No, sir, they are not for sale," said Josiah angrily. He took Dickie's arm and pulled him to his feet. "Come on out of here, Dickie."

But Dickie whimpered, said, "No," and pulled away. "I'm not going there, never, never."

But in the end, Josiah persuaded him to take a look. Dickie mounted Josiah's tall horse and Josiah walked beside him, pointing out the fields belonging to the Home Farm, now green with rye and corn. A field hand waved his hoe at Dickie and roared with laughter, and Dickie said fearfully, "That's Bob Bailey. Ain't he a simpleton?"

"He's a good man with a hoe," said Josiah.

In the farmhouse, he took Dickie into the parlor, where old dames were knitting socks and a couple of old men were bent over a checkerboard. Then he showed Dickie the bustling kitchen and the dining hall and the small sleeping corner he would have to himself.

No longer did Dickie talk of lying down by the side of the road. Next day, he moved in willingly, arriving in a borrowed cart laden with tools and the tag ends of boards. In a back room of the farmhouse he set up a workbench, and soon he was furnishing the Home Farm with cabinets and wardrobes, tables and chairs.

His specialty was elaborate decoration—carved moldings and heraldic devices, finials and crests. Dickie had once made a dressing table for Ingeborg Biddle, the wife of the preacher. To Ingeborg, it had seemed an act of charity. But where on earth had the poor old soul seen sphinxes and classical pilasters and Ionic capitals? The man was illiterate. He didn't even know the going price for that sort of craftsmanship, and really, his work was quite remarkable. Eagerly, Mrs. Biddle had suggested decorative motifs for her dressing table—dimpled cherubs, festoons of flowers. But when the work was done, she had refused to pay for it, because sly Dickie had festooned her pretty table with gargoyles and bats. The cherubs and flowers were now the wonder of the Nashoba Home Farm.

Ingeborg

Ingeborg Biddle

The Reverend Horatio Biddle

As shepherd of all the orthodox Christians in Nashoba, the Reverend Horatio Biddle regarded the occupants of the asylum as part of his flock. And in the opinion of his wife, Ingeborg, he had a higher mandate over their spiritual welfare than did Josiah Gideon, who merely attended to their physical needs. Even so, it was infuriating that Josiah should send some of his poor wretches across the green to occupy three entire pews in Horatio's church every Sunday morning, to disturb the peace of public prayer with their meaningless jabber. Sly! It was a sly insult on Josiah's part. And his costly almshouse was the most grandiose in Middlesex County. Ingeborg considered it her duty to inspect it, to see how extravagantly that dangerous man was wasting the town funds.

When she knocked on the front door of the Nashoba Home Farm, it was opened by a barefoot child—one of the bastards, no doubt—and Josiah came at once. With a courtly bow, he exclaimed, "Welcome, Mrs. Biddle," and led her on a grand tour.

They began in the kitchen, where the matron and the cook rose from their chairs to be introduced, then sat down again to go on with their accounts.

"May I see?" asked Ingeborg sweetly.

The matron looked at her gravely, then handed over the book with its list of the orders for the day:

$14.03	2 bbls. flour
9.31	18 lbs. tea
11.94	120 lbs. cheese

Ingeborg handed it back with a winning smile, then followed Josiah to the dining room, where two orphan female children were clattering plates down on the table. Then she followed him to the common room, where a madwoman screamed at her joyfully and a humpbacked old lady looked up from her tatting and an ancient man sat snoring with his toothless head thrown back. The old gentleman was sitting in an *upholstered chair*, noted Ingeborg, and the towering cabinet in the corner was crowned with a pediment in the Grecian taste, obviously the work of Dickie Doll.

Her kettle had reached the boiling point, but Ingeborg said nothing to Josiah. "Good afternoon, ma'am," he said graciously as she swept out the door.

Only at home could she open the stopcock of her anger. "Are those people to be treated like kings and queens? Before long—are you listening to me, Horatio?—all the old paupers in the surrounding towns will be clamoring to get in. Can't you do something about it, Horatio?"

Her husband looked up from his book in a daze. "About what, my dear?"

"The new almshouse—it's outrageous. Those old women, why can't they earn their keep by taking in washing?"

"It was the selectmen," said Horatio. "Josiah mesmerized the selectmen and the overseers of the poor, and this is the result. The man's a sorcerer."

"And an unbeliever," said Ingeborg. "Don't forget that, Horatio."

Mrs. Ingeborg Biddle was no fool. She had attended a female academy. She had studied German and Italian, algebra, geology, and botany. She had collected minerals and made a herbarium of dried leaves. She also painted china and sang arias in Italian.

And like her scholarly husband, Horatio, she was an ardent disciple of the teachings of Louis Agassiz. It was Professor Agassiz who had explained the Book of Genesis as a beautiful parable. The seven days of creation were a metaphor for God's loving interference in the world. With a slowly improving hand, Professor Agassiz's benevolent God had brought to perfection one species after another, until the whole world displayed the luxuriance of His infinite creative power.

Therefore, it was intolerable that anyone calling himself a Christian clergyman should declare that all creatures on earth had come into being by a series of accidents, and, furthermore, that even the greatest glory of creation, man himself (and woman, too, of course), could be traced back to some howling creature of the jungle.

The *Conversazione*

The town of Nashoba could not, like Concord, boast a nest of philosophers, but it was more than a rural backwater. It had its own lofty pretensions.

It was true that Ingeborg Biddle chafed at the primitive nature of Nashoba society. She often wished that Horatio occupied a pulpit in a town where no hint of a pigsty wafted in the window and no chorus of crowing cocks fractured the peace of the morning, and, above all, where the advancement of womankind was not a terrifying new idea.

Ingeborg herself was an ardent disciple of the movement for female suffrage. While her husband looked backward to the classics of Greece and Rome, Ingeborg was a woman of the future. She revered Miss Fuller's *Woman in the Nineteenth Century.*

She laughed at a timid friend who declared that she would never read George Eliot's *Adam Bede.*

"But why ever not, Elfrida?"

"Why not? Because that woman's personal life is a disgrace." Oh, yes, it was too bad. The women of Nashoba were old-fashioned and conservative. They knew nothing of Miss Fuller's famous defense of the ambitions of women, "Let them be sea-captains, if you will." But these ladies were all that Ingeborg had to work with, so let her instruction begin here.

Therefore, once a month she played hostess in her sitting room to something she called a *conversazione.* These uplifting afternoons were not sewing circles or gossip sessions, but feasts of intellect. Only the more thoughtful ladies of the parish had been invited. Most of her guests were women of mature experience, like Elfrida Poole, but young Ella Viles had been included for her ornamental contribution.

The theme for today had been announced last time. The women had already pondered it gravely at home—whether life's sorrows be not blessings in disguise. Thus the talk began as usual at a high level, but almost at once, to Ingeborg's surprise, it descended from cloudy abstraction to a single naked example: the dreadful affliction that had fallen upon the family of Josiah Gideon.

"Hardly a blessing in their case," said Minnie Wilder, the wife of the postmaster.

"More of a judgment," agreed Elfrida Poole.

Ingeborg thanked her lucky stars that Julia Gideon had not accepted her invitation to join the circle. Julia was certainly one of the more intelligent women of the parish, but her presence this afternoon would have silenced the free exchange of thought.

Abandoning at once her role as captain of a ship tossing in a sea of philosophical speculation, Ingeborg leaned forward boldly and asked the question that was in everyone's mind. "Has anyone actually *seen* him?"

There was a general shudder. "They say," whispered Eugenia

Hunt, "that the poor boy has no lower jaw. *No lower jaw whatso-ever.*"

There were exclamations of horror and pity, and then every-one was relieved when Ingeborg's fluffy cat sauntered into the room. Ingeborg swooped him up, dumped him in the hall, slammed the door, and signaled to Ella Viles to pour the tea. It was unnecessary to say anything more, to point out the conclu-sion of the afternoon's discussion, because it was as plain as the nose on your face.

But as Ella fluttered prettily to the tea table, Cynthia Smith said it out loud. "It's a judgment. That poor young soldier's condition is a judgment on the eccentric behavior of his father-in-law."

"And just think of the soldier's wife," said Ella Viles. "Poor Isabelle!"

"Oh yes," agreed the others, "poor, *dear* Isabelle."

Now, amid the clatter of teacups and the excited chatter of her guests, it was clear to Ingeborg that the afternoon was a suc-cess, another example of the uplifting power of a *conversazione*.

Rise up, ye women of Athens! To the masthead, sea-captains all!

The Scarred Soul of Ingeborg Biddle

Julia Gideon

Yes, Ingeborg's intellectual afternoons were successful, but there was a nagging scar on her soul. Why was it that Julia Gideon refused to join the select circle in her sitting room? Julia's husband, Josiah, was indeed a thorn in Horatio's flesh, but Ingeborg was well aware that it was Josiah's wife, Julia, rather than herself, who was the queen of Nashoba society.

Cruelly etched on Ingeborg's soul was the memory of Julia standing in her doorway, reaching out her arms to poor weeping Dora Whipple after Dora's little son was drowned in the bottomless depths of Quarry Pond. Why hadn't Dora come running for consolation to the wife of her own pastor? Ingeborg would have embraced her just as warmly, soothed her just as tenderly.

And this sort of thing had happened more than once. It was painfully evident that the women of the parish flocked to Julia Gideon in their times of trouble. And now—oh, how it hurt!—in Julia's own time of affliction, she had rejected Ingeborg's sympathy.

Even Horatio had been slighted. As the kindly shepherd of his flock, he had called on the family at once, as soon as it was known that Isabelle and her mutilated husband had come home. But to Horatio's surprise, he had not been permitted to kneel in prayer at the sufferer's bedside.

But surely, thought Ingeborg, the pastor's wife would be less threatening. On the day after Horatio's failure, she had bustled down the hill past the burial ground and across the road, eager to clasp Isabelle in her arms and offer a loving hand of friendship to Julia, the unhappy mother-in-law.

But how had she been received? At the door, Julia Gideon had stood like a stick in her embrace. Ingeborg had been invited into the front room, but no lamp had been lighted for her, and no welcoming fire had been kindled in the parlor stove.

Bravely, Ingeborg had held out her pretty bouquet. "My first daffodils, Julia dear. May I give them to your son-in-law?" But Julia had merely looked down and said nothing. Then Ingeborg had leaned forward and whispered as one woman to another, "I assure you, my dear, I will not flinch."

At this, Julia had shot up out of her chair, reached for the flowers, and said curtly, "Thank you. I will give them to James."

And that was all. Ingeborg had dithered for a moment, then taken her leave.

But her curiosity had been fueled. She was determined to know the true nature of the Gideons' shame, to behold the actual mutilated face of poor Lieutenant Shaw. Somehow or other, she would find a way.

The Dolphin Lady

In spite of the absence of Julia Gideon, Ingeborg Biddle's *conversaziones* were a social triumph. But their success was partly due to the presence in her house of a distinguished secret. Its name was "the Dolphin."

Ingeborg's Dolphin was not one of the appointments of her sitting room, so elegantly furnished with a Kidderminster carpet, a landscape of the Roman *campagna,* Raphael's *Madonna of the Chair,* an Eastlake sofa, and a stereopticon with views of the Pyramid of Cheops.

The Dolphin was sequestered upstairs behind a closed door. It was not the only ornament of that hygienic domain, because Ingeborg was the daughter of the vice president of the J. L. Mott Iron Works of New York City, and therefore she had been privileged to choose freely from their sumptuous catalog.

All of the fixtures had names. The tub was "the Elizabethan" and the lavatory "the Nonpareil." But the glory of all glories was the front-outlet washout ventilating water closet, called "the Dolphin" because the bowl was supported by a porcelain fish tinted with turquoise and gold.

One did not speak of bathroom fixtures in polite company, but Ingeborg could not help smiling when every lady in attendance at one of her conversational tea parties excused herself and disappeared, returning wide-eyed a moment later.

Thus, it was neither the death of Socrates nor the essays of Emerson that were chattered about at home; it was the Dolphin.

If people snickered at Ingeborg behind her back, referring to her as "the Dolphin lady," they were envious just the same. Indoor plumbing was still a rarity in Nashoba. Outhouses were attached to some of the houses, but the usual Nashoba privy stood at the end of a well-worn path.

One afternoon, Ingeborg's Dolphin provided her with a plan. As she pulled the chain, hauled up her drawers, and smoothed down her skirt, she was struck by an idea, and laughed with delight.

It was clear that the house of Julia and Josiah Gideon was not blessed with indoor waterworks, because the pump in the front yard was clearly visible from the road. Undoubtedly, there was an outhouse in the back. An outhouse. If Josiah Gideon, his wife, Julia, and daughter, Isabelle, found it necessary to retire to the backyard privy from time to time, so also would the other occupant of the residence, the disfigured veteran who refused to show his face. It was a law of nature that could not be denied.

The Seat of
the Scornful

The tower of Nashoba's First Parish Church had been intended, like all church steeples, to represent the upward
longing of the spirit, the flight of the soul, the bridge between
earth and heaven. Ingeborg Gideon's use of this modest steeple
as a platform for spying on a neighboring privy was bizarre, but
the sacred symbolism of her perch did not concern her. She sat
on a stack of Sabbath school Bibles in the bell chamber, hoping
to catch a glimpse of the disfigured son-in-law of Josiah Gideon
as he made his way to the outhouse. Even from the attic of the
parsonage, the rear premises of Josiah's property were hidden by
the chestnut tree. Only from the church steeple could she see
the backyard of the house in which the unhappy young man
was hidden away.

The tower also opened up a delightful view of the entire town of Nashoba. Looking down from her high perch, Ingeborg had to admit that it was a pretty little village. The elms planted on the green by the Ornamental Tree Association were still only saplings, but one day they would arch high above the housetops. At this moment, stonemasons were at work in the middle of the green, constructing the pedestal for a war memorial. Concord had erected an obelisk, but Nashoba's was to be a statue. There beside the pedestal lay the little stone soldier, rigidly clutching his rifle. Beyond the memorial, a few young ladies were setting up a game of croquet, pounding the hoops into the grass. The gentle tapping of their mallets was soon drowned out by the clashing pots and pans of a tinware peddler and the sharp rattle of a scissors grinder's wheel. Then even these vulgar noises were overwhelmed by the grinding scream of the steam-powered sawmill on the other side of the graveyard.

Ingeborg was indignant. The sawmill was an insult to the ears and an eyesore right here in the middle of town. Then to the noise of the sawmill was added the rumble of the gristmill on the other side of Quarry Pond.

Suddenly, there was a hush as all the machinery stopped at once, and now Ingeborg could hear the tinkle of "The Happy Farmer" floating up from the piano studio of Elfrida Poole. Then the quiet was fractured once more as the engine of the Nashoba Steam Fire Society started up with a roar. The jolly volunteer firemen were playing with their new toy from New Hampshire, a shining contraption with the words *Fire King* painted on the side. As Ingeborg watched in dismay, the Fire King huffed and puffed and shot a stream of water high in the air. It crested like a fountain and fell on the green like a shower of rain, sending the young ladies ducking away from their game of croquet, stumbling over wickets and shrieking. Ingeborg was mortified. The fools called it practicing, but they were shouting with laughter.

Now she shifted on her stack of Bibles to look westward toward the commercial center of Nashoba. Twenty years ago, when Horatio had accepted the call of the local congregation, the main street had boasted only a smithy, a grain merchant, a harness maker, a grocer, and a butcher, but now it was as up-and-coming as the Milldam in Concord. Sidewalks lined the street, and in the Hubbard Block, a gentleman's haberdasher was doing a thriving business. The Nashoba Mercantile Bank occupied quarters between the post office and the law offices of Peabody and Brown. A livery stable supplied horses, carts, and buggies for hire, and a dry-goods store was stocked with a delightful assortment of sewing materials for the women of Nashoba—bolts of poplin, broadcloth, and French cassimere, as well as velvets, silks, and every sort of ruching, fringe, and braid. Regrettably, there was also a tavern at the end of the street, the Rising Sun.

With a creak of her stays, Ingeborg turned sideways and craned her neck the other way. From here, she could see children emerging from the district school, escaping from Euclid's *Elements* and the baggage trains of Julius Caesar. But the ornament of the village was housed in the Wheeler Block, the Nashoba Social Library. Not only did the library possess a thousand books; it also boasted a cabinet of minerals, the gift of Ingeborg Biddle. The most constant borrower of reading matter was Ingeborg herself—that is, after one other person.

"I suppose, Maria," Ingeborg had said to the librarian, "that I am the worst offender in emptying your shelves of books. Forgive me, dear."

"Oh, no, rest easy, Mrs. Biddle. You're not nearly so bad as Mrs. Gideon."

Ingeborg winced, remembering the insult. But it wasn't the views to east and west that were of interest to her now. Swiveling once again on her Bibles, she looked south to the house in which Julia Gideon was said to be reading even more books than Ingeborg Biddle. It did not occur to Ingeborg that within the tattered Bibles crushed beneath her stays was the Book of Psalms with its blessing on "the man that walketh not in the counsel of the ungodly, nor sitteth in the seat of the scornful."

Scornful indeed was her seat, but this morning her observation seemed futile. It was laundry day in the Gideon household. Their backyard was a cloud of billowing sheets. *Did that nightshirt belong to the monster?*

Ingeborg hitched forward on her pyramid of Old and New Testaments. Who were those people pulling up in front of the house in a high-seated gig? Oh, of course, it was Dr. Clock. The woman beside him must be his wife, Ida. The small boy jumping down from her lap was surely too old to be the fruit of this marriage. He must be the child of her first husband, *the deserter.* How kind of the doctor to raise the boy as his own!

Ingeborg watched as Dr. Clock was welcomed into the house by Josiah's daughter. Then she was surprised to see that instead of inviting the doctor's wife and little stepson into the house, Isabelle ran out to join them. Ingeborg watched as Isabelle kissed Ida, hugged the little boy, and patted the horse's nose.

Patiently, Ingeborg waited for the end of the doctor's visit. At last, he came hurrying out of the house and mounted the gig. At once, the horse started up with a sprightly bounce, nearly tossing the little boy over the side. The doctor grabbed him by the strap of his overalls, flicked his whip, and immediately horse and wagon were off and away, rattling down the turnpike on the way home to Concord.

Surely now the women of the Gideon household would be free to do something about the tossing sheets in the backyard. Ingeborg stared impatiently. Why on earth didn't someone take them in? By now, they must certainly be bone-dry. The enormous chestnut tree shaded the front of the house, but the sheets in the backyard flapped in the sunshine.

Ingeborg was tired of her vigil. Frustration made her bold. What if she were to walk down the hill and wander behind the house as though looking for her fluffy gray pussy? Why ever not!

Carefully, she picked up her skirts and made her way down the ladder to the platform where the ticking clockworks smelled of machine oil, and then down a staircase to the vestry. Here she brushed her skirts, patted her high-piled curls, and walked down the hill. With a dignified step, she strolled past the front of the Gideon house and turned the corner on Quarry Pond Road to observe the ménage from the side. But there were too many tall bushes. Darting a glance left and right, Ingeborg slipped in among the lilacs. The path to the privy was still out of sight. Boldly, she pushed branches aside, until at last she could see the back door, the path, and the latticed bower enclosing the outhouse.

But then she had a fright. An orange cat, a clawing cat, a cat that was not her fluffy gray pussy, leaped out of the bushes and landed on her shoulder. Ingeborg screamed and sprawled full length across the path just as Josiah Gideon emerged from the outhouse.

Gallantly, he helped her to her feet. "Madam," he said, throwing wide the privy door, "I beg you to be my guest."

NOW

The Lost Steeple

Lost, lost is the music! Lost
All the prayers and the people!

Lost Is the Music

I 've been thinking," said Mary, thumping down her empty beer glass on the kitchen table.

"Dangerous habit," said Homer. "What about?"

"About the great unwashed. I mean in history."

"The great unwashed?" Homer snickered and wrenched open another bottle. "I worry more about the great washed. I hate the way everybody nowadays is so clean. They brush their teeth and gargle away their foul breath, and shampoo their hair until it's squeaky-clean, and all the women shave their legs and all the men frustrate the urge of every whisker on their chins to emerge into the light, and that isn't all. After purifying their bodies, they attack their brains with wire brushes and cleansing powder until everything of interest has been scrubbed away."

"But, Homer, that's exactly what I mean. When you think about history—"

"Unless, of course, it's sexual intercourse," Homer went on, correcting himself. "That stuff never goes away."

"Sexual intercourse?" Mary looked blank, then hurtled on. "Okay, but I've been thinking about history. Cleanliness wasn't so rife in the past. Listen, Homer, what about all those great dead people? You know, the Shakespeares and Johann Sebastian Bachs and the Walt Whitmans and the Wordsworths of times gone by. They weren't squeaky-clean. They didn't have the plumbing for it, or maybe they didn't even feel the need."

"Thoreau was clean," objected Homer primly. "At Walden, he bathed in the pond every day."

"Well, good for Henry, but what about the others? We look at these great icons from afar, but what if we came close, really close, very, very close? What would they be like? Think of the foul latrines and the greasy bedding. Think of the dirty feet and the unwashed bodies. Think of the bad breath and the spitting, the stinking underwear, the rotting garbage and the excrement thrown into the street. Think of the privies! You know, Homer, there were still a few privies in Concord when I was a little girl."

Homer flinched. "I see what you mean. The great and glorious unwashed." Shuddering, he changed the subject. "Guess what? I've slipped again."

"Slipped? Oh, you mean—"

"The bestseller list. I've sunk to fifth place."

"Well, fifth place isn't so bad. You just have to get the new book out in a hurry. Wait a sec, Homer; you've got to see this." Mary reached for her notebook and flapped the pages back and forth. "It's sort of mysterious and exciting. Maybe you could work it in. Did you ever hear of a lost church around here anywhere?"

"A lost church?" Homer grinned. "How could a church get itself lost?"

She sucked her pencil. "I know it sounds strange."

"You mean it just pointed its steeple at the horizon and took off, galumphing away in the night?"

"Heaven knows. I was bumbling around in the archives of the Concord Library and I found something strange. I wouldn't have paid any attention to one crazy letter, but there were two of them. Look, here's the first one. It was just a wisp of torn paper in a file. No date, no return address, no signature. I made a copy. Look."

Homer looked. The handwriting was old-fashioned but precise. It started in the middle of a sentence:

> . . . *picnicking with my dear friends from Concord, Honoria and Mary Ann. Now Mother you know what alwayz happens at picnics it began to pore pitchforks so we went into the empty church and I found a hym book under a bench so I took it because nobody comes there now.*

Homer shook his head. "This is your lost church? But, Mary, it could be anyplace. Her dear friends were from Concord, but maybe the letter was written from someplace else entirely. And maybe it was the other Concord, the one in New Hampshire."

"Yes, that's what I thought. But then I found this." Mary turned a page. "This one has a date."

> *July 17, '69*
>
> *Dearest Honey,*
>
> *Our Poetry Social met yesterday and my little offering was well received! In fact (forgive me, dearest, for bragging) our President praised it as worthy of Oliver Wendell Holmes himself! Think of that!*

THE LOST CHURCH

Deep in the forest primeval
And shrouded in shrubbery,
A prey to woodworm and weevil,
The empty church stands.

No sermon of good or of evil
Resounds from that pulpit.
No minister's eloquent hands
Are lifted in blessing.

How many a swift grain of sand
Has drained from the glass
Since last these walls echoed
With hymn music grand?

Lost, lost is the music! Lost
All the prayers and the people!
Lost, tempest-tossed
And forever abandoned,
The little lost church and the steeple.

"What do you think?" said Mary. "Isn't it sweet?"

"The little lost church," said Homer dreamily. "Maybe it was the church of churches, the temple of temples, the perfect union of truth and majesty. I'll bet it was translated."

"Translated? Oh, you mean—"

"Swept up to heaven." Homer lifted his hands in wonder. "It was too good for this world, so now it's up there in paradise, an alabaster cathedral, with Socrates and Jesus taking turns in the pulpit."

1868

The News from Fairyland

What's the news of the day,
Good neighbour, I pray ?
They say the balloon
Has gone up to the moon.

Mother Goose's Melodies, *1845*

The Mind of Horace

Eudocia Flint

W hen Alexander, Ida, and Horace came home from Nashoba, Eudocia was waiting with baby Gussie in her arms.
Ida stepped down from the buggy and took the baby. Eudocia
lifted Horace down and said, "Were you my good boy?"

"Of course he was," said Ida.

"I saw a big tree," said Horace. He spread his arms wide. "As
big as a giant."

"Oh, yes," said his grandmother, unbuttoning his jacket. "I
know that big tree."

Jake peered over the side of the basket as the balloon wafted
over Walden Pond. "You see Hector anyplace, Jack?"

"He's a-comin', Jake," said Jack. "See him down there in the wagon, galloping that old horse? Whoopsie, Jake! Look at that. Wheel fell off the wagon."

Jake looked down at the disaster on the Walden Road and said mildly, "It's all right, Jack. Horse ain't dead. Hector'll catch up by and by."

"You do love him a little?" Ida whispered to Alexander as she lay beside him in the big bed that had once belonged to her mother and father.

"Of course," said Alexander, "just as I love his mother. And after all, who was it who helped bring Horace into the world?"

Ida smiled as she rested in the crook of her husband's arm. It was true that Horace had been born in the Patent Office hospital in Washington, where Alexander Clock had been chief surgeon. Ida had gone looking for her husband, Seth, missing after the Battle of Gettysburg. Instead, she had found her sixteen-year-old brother, Eben, deathly ill with typhoid fever. Then instead of going home to Concord to have her baby, she had stayed to help care for her brother. And therefore when her pains began, the head nurse had been forced, willy-nilly, to find her a bed.

But was it true that Alexander had helped with the baby's birth? No, of course it wasn't true. Although army surgeon Alexander Clock had been acquainted with every kind of war-time casualty, he had known nothing whatever about babies. He had seen the infant born and he had watched with relief as baby Horace was handed to his mother, and then he had visited the pretty pair every day for the next week, while Eben recovered in another part of the hospital. And when the little family had packed up its belongings and left for home, Dr. Clock had written to Ida every day. Her search for Seth had ended with the news of his death, and now it was Alexander who lay beside her in the bed in which she had been born.

But Horace was no longer an only child. He had a half sister, Augusta, who was still nursing at her mother's breast. Everyone fussed over Gussie. Nobody fussed over Horace. Every night, the house was loud with Gussie's cries. Every day, it steamed with Gussie's washing. There were kettles boiling on the stove, set tubs sloshing with soapy water, hands rough and red from rubbing small garments on scrubbing boards, and on wet days Gussie's laundry stretched across the kitchen and flapped in Horace's face. And yet, after causing all this trouble, Gussie was the one who was kissed and cooed over, not Horace.

It was clear to his grandmother that Horace's small nose was out of joint. Therefore, Eudocia adopted him as her special charge. "Come, Horace dear," she would say when he was scolded for misbehaving, "I'll read you the story of Goldilocks and the three bears." Or sometimes it was nursery rhymes— "Humpty-Dumpty" and "Little Boy Blue" and all the rest. Horace sopped them up. He lived in them; they filled his head with pictures.

So for five-year-old Horace Morgan, the world was populated by elves and fairies, gnomes and trolls, storekeepers on the Milldam, giants and goose girls, white rabbits and the spotted cow, the man in the moon, his mother and grandmother, Little Jack Horner, and the horses in the stable.

Therefore, when the hot-air balloon of the brothers Spratt drifted over the apple orchard, Horace was not surprised. The fantastic spectacle was all of a piece with the floating gossamer of dandelions and the news from fairyland.

The Tinkerer

In the busy household of Eudocia Flint on the road to Barrett's mill, Horace was surrounded by young aunts and uncles. Josh and Alice were still children, but Sallie was seventeen and Eben older still. At twenty-one, he was his mother's right-hand man. Eben's brother-in-law was older, of course, but Alexander was often miles away, attending a sickbed.

Therefore, Eben was in charge of the heavy chores around the place. It was no longer a working farm, unless two horses, a cow, and miscellaneous poultry made it a farm, but like every boy brought up in the country, Eben could handle just about anything, from daily chores to unexpected calamities like the one last week: a raid on the henhouse by a fox. He had been forced to drop everything and mend the fence, while his mother wept over the carcass of the Toulouse goose, then got to work plucking and roasting it and rendering the fat in a kettle.

The care of the apple trees had been abandoned, "at least for now," said Eudocia regretfully, remembering an orchard cloudy with blossoms and heavy with fruit. But there was still a great deal to do. Hay had to be cut with a reaping machine borrowed from Mr. Hosmer, and stored in the hayloft. Trees had to be felled in the woodlot, carted home, and split for the stove, and now and then a few cedars from the farthest field were hewn into fence posts. The cow had to be milked twice a day and taken to the bull once a year, and her calf safely delivered in the spring. Of course, some supplies had to be brought from town, oats and flour from the grain merchant, lamp oil, sugar and soap from Cutler's store, as well as luxuries from all over the world—raisins from the Levant, tea from China, oranges from Spain.

Eben's mother did most of the cooking and the laundry, although Ida handled her baby's washing and Sallie helped with the shirts, slamming down one heavy iron on the stove and picking up another. Little Alice helped out in the kitchen, obeying the sharp commands of the whirlwind that was her mother, as Eudocia darted from flour bin to bread board, pried up stove lids to poke at the fire, disemboweled a hen, slammed a butcher knife down on a side of pork, or jerked open an oven door to pull out a loaf pan, her hand bunched in her apron.

Eben took his household chores for granted, but Josh was apt to use bad words while shoveling out the slimy heaps plopped in the gutter by the cow. Sallie had been known to burst into tears at the sight of the laundry piled high in the basket, and Alice sometimes dropped dishes on purpose.

As for Horace, Eben's five-year-old nephew never complained about his chore of finding new-laid eggs in the henhouse, although he often broke as many as he carried safely inside to his grandmother.

Eben's real employment was away from home. Six days a week, he took the cars to Waltham, where he was employed as a draftsman for a firm of church architects. His school days were over, but Eben's two years of study at the college in Cambridge had included not only orations in Latin and Greek but chemical experiments—inflating bubbles with hydrogen, making light with phosphorus, as well as the precise recording of the results. Now he was equally precise in the drafting of architectural plans and elevations, although he didn't much care for the fussy designs of his employer. He was eager to try his hand at something of his own.

It was a common saying, Every farmer a mechanic. It was certainly true of Eben, who had a Yankee knack for tinkering. His boyish perpetual-motion machine had failed to work, but his waterwheel had turned an axle that twirled a paper bird. Now he took on a project for his wounded friend James Shaw.

"The trouble with these hooks of yours," he told James, "is that they don't grip. You need to pick things up and hold them." When James made a mournful sound and shook his head, Eben said, "No, James, truly. I swear I can do it."

And within the week, he was back with a gadget that squeezed and let go, and squeezed again. James lifted his hooked stumps in despair.

"Please, James," said Isabelle. "Let Eben try it."

"It isn't perfect yet," said Eben, opening and shutting the contraption. "You'll need help at first. But once it closes on a spoon, you'll be able to feed yourself. Or hold a pen tightly enough to write."

"Oh, yes, James," said Isabelle eagerly. "Here, let's try."

But the first holding device refused to be attached to the stump of James's right arm. "No matter," said Eben cheerfully. "I can see what's wrong. I'll try again."

At the door, Isabelle took his hand. "You are a such a good friend to James. He would thank you if he could."

Eben had known Isabelle at school, where she had been the shyest girl in the seventh grade. His mother and father had known Isabelle's mother and father. But now, although it no longer troubled Eben to look at James, he was afraid to look at Isabelle. The crisis was too great and her trouble too crushing to give him any right to look at her. Turning away, he put on his hat. "I'll be back on Sunday, if it's no trouble."

"Of course not," said Isabelle, and she went back to James.

"Where were we, James?" she said, picking up *A Tale of Two Cities.* "Oh, I remember." Sitting down beside him, she began to read. " *'Good night, citizen,' said Sydney Carton. 'How goes the Republic?'* " Isabelle paused before reading the sawyer's response. " *'You mean the Guillotine. Not ill. Sixty-three to-day. We shall mount to a hundred soon.'* "

One of the Noblest
Works of God

The giant tree that straddled the stone wall at the bottom of the Nashoba burial ground had already been growing on this hillside when the tribe of Nipmucks came from the north to fish at the junction of the rivers and hunt in the forest of the countryside known as Nashoba. Some of them had been "praying Indians," but all of them, whether converted to Christianity or not, would have seen the branches of the chestnut tree hung with fragrant yellow flowers in summer. And they would have gathered the harvest of nuts that rained down in the fall, just as throngs of children did now, appearing like magic under the tree to fill pockets and baskets and pails.

The chestnut tree was massively broad and tall, rising from its gnarled platform like a monument from a pedestal. Some of its branches were dead and bare, but new shoots had sprung up to become part of the whole, and now the entire tree was sprightly with fresh green leaves. Whenever Josiah Gideon left his front door, he gave it an admiring glance.

This morning as he came out to prime the pump and fill a pitcher, Josiah looked across the road and saw Horatio Biddle standing under the tree. Josiah set the pitcher on the doorstep, walked across the road, and climbed over the wall to say good morning. Then the two clergymen, neighbors on this hillside and—whatever Ingeborg Biddle might say—colleagues in the ministry, stood side by side under the tree, contemplating the magnificent spread of leaf and branch over their heads. As always, the sight exhilarated Josiah. He wanted to exclaim, but he refrained.

Then the man beside him made a remark. "See there, it's cracked the monument to Deacon Sweetser."

Josiah lowered his eyes down and down, through layer after green layer, to the foot of the tree, where the slate tombstone of old Deacon Sweetser stood tall and tilted, heaved to one side by the thick mass of interwoven roots.

"It won't do," said Horatio Biddle. "And anyhow, that tree's too old. Next big wind, the whole thing will fall down."

Josiah looked at him keenly. "It hasn't fallen yet."

"No, but it's bound to happen." Horatio whistled for a moment, then clapped his hands and made a pronouncement. "That tree must be removed."

"You're jesting," said Josiah.

"No, no, it must come down."

"Come down?" Josiah was dumbfounded. "Surely you don't mean it? Look here, Horatio, I have a better idea. Why not move Deacon Sweetser instead?"

"Move Deacon Sweetser? Profane a Christian burial?" Horatio Biddle was shocked in his turn. "Remove a casket from the place where it was reverently interred a century ago? My dear Josiah, have you no respect for the dead? That is an abominable suggestion." Horatio dismissed the idea with a wave of his hand, turned away, and said once again, "The tree must come down."

"No," cried Josiah. "Horatio, you wouldn't do anything so outrageous."

Pausing to look back, Horatio said patiently, "Calm yourself, Josiah," and glanced up again at the tree. "Lord God in heaven, that trunk must be eight or nine feet across."

"Because it's so old," shouted Josiah. "That tree's a lot older than Deacon Sweetser. What about respect for one of the noblest works of God?"

"Nonsense," said Horatio, stalking away up the hill. "I've made up my mind." He did not tell Josiah his next resolve, which was to act promptly, before the fool had time to arouse sympathy among the other members of the congregation.

True, the chestnut tree was old, but it was only a tree after all. What mattered a tree compared with the long and upright life of that pious old father of the Nashoba church, Deacon Joseph Sweetser? Through all the ages to come, his old bones would remain where they were, until the Last Day and the thundering knock on the coffin lid.

Shovels and Spades

Julia Gideon was reading aloud by lantern light. *"Along the Paris streets, the death-carts rumble, hollow and harsh. Six tumbrils carry the day's wine to La Guillotine."* Raising her eyes from the book, Julia looked across the room. Had James fallen asleep?

No, he was turning his head on the pillow to look at her. His single eye was dark and brilliant in the lantern light, but once again he pulled the sheet over the rest of his ruined face. Julia remembered the way her old father had covered his mouth to hide his toothless jaw. She murmured, "Can you sleep now, James?"

He nodded, but she guessed it was a lie. When Isabelle came into the room in her nightdress, her hair falling down her back, Julia laid the book on the table, whispered good night, and turned to go. But then she had to stand aside for her husband and Eben Flint.

In the lantern light, their faces loomed up out of the dark hall. "Hello, Eben," said Isabelle, feeling her cheeks grow warm.

Eben gazed at her for a startled moment, then backed away in confusion. Josiah struck a match and lighted a candle. He handed it to his wife, picked up the lantern, and gave her a flashing look. "We need it outside. Don't wait up. We may be gone awhile."

Something in her husband's face alarmed Julia, but she took the candle and said nothing. The floor creaked under two pairs of boots and the circle of light moved away, leaving only the candle.

Soon there were noises from the shed, soft clinkings and clashings. James lifted his head and Julia went to the window with Isabelle. Moving the curtain aside, they saw Josiah and Eben emerge from the shed. The lantern in Eben's hand made silhouettes of the long-handled tools on their shoulders.

Shovels and spades. What were they doing out-of-doors in the dark of night with shovels and spades?

Deacon Sweetser Moves North

Perhaps Horatio Biddle had been born a clergyman, babbling sermons in his cradle and waving his little fists in declamatory gestures. Now as a grown man, he felt himself to be the natural lord of his congregation. Ever since the laying on of hands at the time of his ordination, he had been the spiritual master of his flock. In that instant, he had become the inheritor of an ancestral line of Christian preachers. Every hand that had lain upon his head had belonged to a clergyman who had himself received just such a laying on of hands by older men of God, and they, too, had been blessed by the hands of an earlier generation. The ceremony of ordination was a passing of spiritual authority from one age to the next, a solemn succession going back and back in time.

But on the morning following the dark midnight when Josiah Gideon and Eben Flint had set off with their shovels and spades, Horatio Biddle woke up and beheld a horrid defiance of his inherited authority. As he pulled off his nightcap and yawned and glanced out the window, he saw something entirely unexpected. A tombstone was standing at the top of the burial ground in a place where no tombstone had stood before.

Horatio threw up the sash and leaned out to stare down the hill to the place where the chestnut tree rose splendidly in the sweet morning air, its great limbs spreading far and high, its constellations of new leaves translucent in the light of the rising sun. He could see no trace of the resting place of Deacon Sweetser below the tree. There was no ugly pit in the ground, no visible scar. It was as though the venerable deacon had never slept at the foot of the chestnut tree.

Outraged, Horatio threw on his clothes in such a hurry that his wife sat up in bed and complained, "Good gracious, Horatio, your shirt's on inside out."

"No matter." Her husband charged out of the bedroom, thundered down the stairs, threw open the door, and raced across the green through the dew-wet grass, then pounded along a quiet street, past a sleepy boy carrying a bucket into a cowshed and past the house of the widow Whittey, who was at that moment sweeping her front stoop. Miss Whittey looked up at Horatio and dropped her broom, but he charged past her without a word and rounded the corner to a path that meandered away from the road. The path led to an untidy yard full of sawbucks and to the shack that was the home of two brothers, Brendan and Daniel Fitzmorris. They were sawyers.

Horatio sometimes pitied the foreign element in town, but the Fitzmorris brothers were not within his charge, since they were Irish Catholics. The kindly reach of parish charity did not extend to papists, no matter how needy they might be. Now, at least, they would be paid for laboring in a Protestant cause. Their saws and axes owed no allegiance to the Pope in Rome.

"You there," cried Horatio Biddle, pounding on the shanty door. "Wake up."

By ten o'clock in the morning of the same day, across Nashoba Brook in the town of Concord, Eudocia Flint and most of her family were up and about. Eben had come home at dawn, but after sleeping only a few hours, he had dragged himself out of bed to go back to Nashoba with Alexander. Baby Gussie was asleep. Ida, too, had been nodding off in the rocking chair until the loud singing voice of her mother jerked her awake.

In the sitting room downstairs, Eudocia's feet vigorously worked the treadles of the reed organ, her fingers bouncing on the keys and her knees thrusting sideways against the levers that sent more air into the bellows. Eudocia's lungs expanded, too, as she gave tongue to a jolly song, "Oh, the bulldog on the bank! And the bullfrog in the pool!"

It was the signal for Horace's music lesson. But when Horace did not run into the room and climb into her lap, Eudocia stood up and called for her grandson, "Horace? Where are you?"

Ida laid Gussie in her cradle and ran downstairs, telling herself that she should have been keeping track of Horace. Any day now, her clever little boy would learn how to draw the bolts on the doors.

"Horace, Horace," called Ida. But at the foot of the stairs, she whispered, "Oh no," because the bolt had been drawn and the door stood wide open.

Eudocia and Ida looked everywhere. Sallie and Josh and Alice scattered to look for the missing boy in the henhouse, the stable, the barn, and the orchard. Naughty Horace was nowhere to be found.

But when the Reverend Horatio Biddle made his way back to the chestnut tree at the foot of the burial ground, accompanied by two men armed with axes and saws, he saw the lost boy high in the branches of the tree, looking down at him and laughing.

The Bulldog and
the Bullfrog

Horace lived at full tilt. His behavior was not the naughtiness of a neglected child. In running out the door, he was
not escaping from a cruel stepfather or an unloving mother. It
was Horace's nature to head for the horizon. Every morning, he
woke up eager to discover what lay beyond the washstand and
the cupboard, beyond the house and the barn and the pasture
fence. His mother was exhausted by the effort of keeping her
five-year-old son in check, but Ida was secretly proud of his
wanderlust. Someday, somehow, she was sure it would take
him far.

To the three big men staring up at the small boy sitting high in
the chestnut tree, Horace presented a quandary.

Brendan Fitzmorris had seen the boy before, and therefore when he caught sight of Dr. Clock and Eben Flint emerging from the house of Josiah Gideon, he shouted at them and pointed up at Horace.

Horatio Biddle watched with satisfaction as the heads of Alexander and Eben swiveled to follow Brendan's pointing hand. Gratified, he saw them cross the road and climb over the wall.

"Is that your boy?" thundered Horatio. He, too, pointed skyward (it was a favorite pulpit gesture).

Alexander and Eben looked up at the chubby object sitting high overhead in the famous chestnut tree. Looking down, they saw the Fitzmorris brothers with their mighty axes and long two-handled saws. Alexander exchanged a glance with Eben, and then, instead of shouting up at Horace and ordering him to come down, he swung himself up on a low branch and began climbing. Eben grinned and followed him. Hand over hand, they went up easily. The branches were like stair steps. Horatio Biddle watched them climb higher and higher, and he smiled at the thought of the scolding the mischievous boy was about to receive.

Horace waited cheerfully for his uncle and stepfather. "I'm all right, Papa," he called down as they came nearer. "I'm all right, Uncle Eben."

There was an angry shout from below: "Get that boy down."

"Of course you're all right, Horace." Alexander smiled at his small stepson and stepped sideways to settle down beside him and hold him firmly with one arm. Eben found a nearby branch, and at once he piped up with a favorite song of his mother's—Eudocia had brought up a singing family. "Oh, the bulldog on the bank!"

At once, Horace and Alexander chimed in with the next line. "And the bullfrog in the pool!"

With the last lines, they were joined by a deep bellow from below. "And the bulldog called the bullfrog a green old water fool!"

Looking down, they saw Josiah Gideon leaping up into the

tree. They watched him climb higher and higher, his strong hands grasping branch after branch, his beard streaming sideways and his great laugh booming all over the graveyard.

Soon there were four birds nesting in the top of the tree. Gazing around the horizon from their lofty perch, Josiah, Eben, Alexander, and Horace could see eight church steeples pointing skyward above the treetops in villages to the east, west, north, and south.

Far below at the foot of the tree, the Fitzmorris brothers were grinning from ear to ear, but the bullfrog was beside himself with rage.

The Perching Birds

Across the street, James Shaw twitched aside the curtain with the hook of his right arm and saw his mother-in-law run out the door to the gate. He made a sound in his throat, and Isabelle came hurrying to him from the kitchen. Looking out, she saw her dignified mother hoisting her skirts and clambering over the stone wall. In the burying ground, three men were looking up into the chestnut tree.

What were they staring at? Isabelle lifted her eyes to the broad green canopy and saw three men and a child perched in it like birds. One of the men was her father. The second was Dr. Clock. The third was Eben Flint. The child was Eben's small nephew, Horace. Quickly, Isabelle kissed James and ran out the door after her mother.

Other women came, too. The news was spreading like wild-fire. Someone had notified Eudocia, and now she came racing along the Concord Road in the spring wagon, accompanied by Ida with baby Augusta bouncing in her arms. Stepping down, Eudocia and Ida left Mab nosing at buttercups. Taking the baby in turns, they helped each other over the wall.

The nature of the melodrama unfolded at once—the men with their axes, the endangered tree, and the fury of the Reverend Horatio Biddle, gazing up at the defiance in the top of the tree.

"Hello, Mama," shouted Horace, waving joyfully. "Hello, Grandmaw."

"Oh, Horace dear," cried Ida, "hang on tight."

"You hear that, Horace?" shouted Eudocia.

"It's all right," called Alexander. "I've got him."

Julia Gideon stared up anxiously at Josiah. She did not call out, but Isabelle shouted, "Father, are you all right?"

Was he all right? Josiah could hardly contain his joy. The tree on which he stood was the embodiment of the great meta-phorical tree "that fills with its dead and broken branches the crust of the earth and covers the surface with its ever-branching and beautiful ramifications." Now, standing at the summit of both at once, the symbolic as well as the actual tree, he could see its long fingering branches reach out beyond the woods and fields and houses of Nashoba and the enclosing horizon of vil-lages and steeples to enclose all the mountains and valleys and seas of the earth, the whole luxuriant terrestrial globe of trees and flowers, birds and beasts. Therefore, instead of answering his daughter, he stretched out one arm in a gesture of exaltation.

Isabelle and Julia, looking up fearfully from below, could see his shining face. Eben, too, seemed transported. Horace crowed with delight, and even sober Alexander was laughing aloud.

Within the hour, a crowd was gathered around the base of the tree, and seventeen eager climbers had mounted into the up-per branches. Even Ella Viles tried to join Eben, but when she tore her pretty sash, she descended timidly.

The tree dwellers chattered and sang. Baskets of tidbits were hoisted up, empty baskets let down. When Horace whispered something to his stepfather in distress, Alexander turned him around to face the other way and undid his buttons. Horace let fly eastward, giggling at the pattering noise on the leaves below.

Meanwhile, Horatio Biddle had been joined by his wife. From the bedroom window of the parsonage, Ingeborg had surveyed the scene in a state of alarm, but now she whispered in his ear, "Over here, Horatio," and led him a little way apart.

Their domestic dialogue did not last long. Soon Ingeborg retreated, smiling. Her husband approached the tree and called up to Josiah and Alexander and Eben and all the others, "All right, gentlemen, you've won. You can all come down."

There were whoops of joy in the high branches overhead. Eben stood up on his branch, reached for Horace, and followed Alexander down, and then all the other tree dwellers came down, too, laughing and calling, appearing and disappearing in the bright universe of sunlit leaves. Only Josiah Gideon remained aloft a moment longer to gaze around at the spreading view of field and woodland, steeple and rooftop. He was the last to set foot on the ground.

Eudocia gathered up Horace and kissed his beaming face, Ida kissed Alexander, Alexander kissed the baby, Ella Viles threw her arms around Eben, and Isabelle hugged her father.

Julia was the only one who thought of thanking Horatio Biddle, but he had strolled away with the Fitzmorris brothers.

"Later," he said to Brendan Fitzmorris. "I'll need you boys later on."

NOW

Another Steeple

*Little of all we value here
Wakes on the morn of its hundredth year
Without both feeling and looking queer.
In fact, there's nothing that keeps its youth,
So far as I know, but a tree and truth.*

—Oliver Wendell Holmes,
"The Wonderful One
Hoss-Shay"

The Weirdness of the Past

Homer had begun to doubt the entire meaning of his life's work. There had been a slippage of faith. What if everything he thought he knew about the past was wrong? What if the present moment slipped into a well as soon as it was over, a well so deep and bottomless that his bucket could only clatter against the stones and come up empty?

Homer got out of the car in the parking lot of Nashoba's Old West Church and stood for a moment on the pavement, staring up at the low dome of the steeple. What exactly was the truth about his own life only a moment ago? Five minutes ago, having forgotten how to find the town green, he had been driving along Quarry Pond Road from the direction of Route 2A, and then he had blundered around Gideon Circle and turned the wrong way on Flint Street, or had it been Gideon Street and Flint Circle? There, you see? You dip your hand in the past and the truth runs through your fingers like water.

So the whole thing was hopeless. The past was weird and unknowable. How could he presume to know anything whatever about a time when every gesture of a hand, every habit of talk, every simple unconscious action was shrouded by the curtains of the years that lay between, each a darker and thicker veil, until everything was blotted out?

Then Homer cheered up, for it occurred to him that architecture was dependable. Buildings hung on comfortably while generations came and went. Infants were carried in to be baptized and eighty years later their coffins were carried out, while the building continued to stand. Old West Church was itself a chunk of the nineteenth century. This solid collection of wood and stone, plaster and glass had been part of Nashoba in the past and it was part of it still.

Mulling over this truism, Homer walked past a sign inviting him to a lecture on "The Archetype of Healing" and found himself in a basement corridor. Here the floorboards were so solid under his feet and so old at the same time that Homer wondered if he might find a wizened deacon entombed in a broom closet or an ancient choirmistress pressed like a flower in a hymnbook.

The Reverend Joseph Bold was very much alive. When Homer knocked on his office door and walked in, the present-day shepherd of Nashoba's Old West Church looked pink and healthy, if slightly harassed. Joe was an old friend, and it didn't take him long to understand the nature of Homer's stumbling questions.

"Oh, I get it," said Joe. "You're looking for dirt, is that it?"

Homer was embarrassed. "Well, I wouldn't call it 'dirt' exactly. Say the sort of gossip that everybody knows at the time, only it never gets into the history books."

"Sorry, Homer," said Joe. "I wish I knew gossip like that.

Sometimes it's the best kind of history. The trouble is, I'm ashamed to say that I don't know much at all about our background, except that we used to be known as the First Parish of Nashoba. That is, until the Universalists set up shop around the corner in the 1880s. So after that, this one's been Old West, even after we joined forces."

Homer was distracted by the framed photograph on the wall. He jumped up to take a look. "Who's this old guy?"

"Some pastor from days gone by. I forget his name." Joe stood up, too, and peered at the spidery writing under the photograph. "The Reverend Horatio Biddle. Oh, sure, I remember him. He's got a tombstone out there in the graveyard."

"Well, it's too bad," said Homer, sinking back in his chair. "I gather you don't have any juicy scandals for me. But that's all right. In fact it's just as well. I'm ashamed of myself for asking. It's not me, Joe, honest it isn't. It's my editor. That's the kind of stuff he wants."

"Now wait a minute, Homer. Hold your horses." Joe frowned. "I think there was a scandal about a tree."

"A tree? A scandal about a tree?"

"Well, maybe. It sounds unlikely. I'm probably wrong."

"Well, how about a lost church?"

"A lost church?"

"I know it sounds ridiculous, but—"

"No, wait." Joe stared fiercely at Homer's whiskers. "A lost church. It strikes a chord."

"It does?" Homer pulled a folder out of his bag and handed Joe the letter with the sentimental poem, the verses about the mysterious church that was "lost, tempest-tossed and forever abandoned."

Joe read the poem aloud. *"Deep in the forest primeval and shrouded in shrubbery, a prey to woodworm and weevil, the empty church stands."* At the end, he looked up at Homer and said, "Goodness me."

"Oh, it was just some amateur poetry group, way back in

1869," said Homer, feeling foolish. "They told this woman it was worthy of Oliver Wendell Holmes. See at the top where it says that?"

"Mmm, yes." Joe stared at the poem and murmured, " *'Lost, lost is the music!'* " Looking up dreamily, he said, "Oliver Wendell Holmes, that's right. There was something about Oliver Wendell Holmes."

"You mean something else about Holmes, not just this poem?"

"I think so." Joe stood up. "Look, Homer, I'm late for a meeting. And anyway, I'm no good to you. The person you ought to speak to is old Miss Flint. She knows more about the history of this church than anybody else."

"Miss Flint?"

"Right. Miss Flint is one of our oldest citizens. In fact, I think she was born here."

"Oh, good, I was hoping you'd have a dear little old lady."

"Dear little old lady?" There was a pause. Joe seemed to have fallen into a reverie. Then he woke up and said thoughtfully, "The fact is, Homer, I've never met the woman. I gather she's something of a recluse. She lives out on Acton Road on the corner of Route Two A. You know, right behind the pizza place. You know the pizza place?"

"Can't say I do."

"Well, that's where she lives. I tried to call on her once—you know, the new clergyman in town making polite pastoral calls on all the old folks and shut-ins." Joe shook his head. "But there was a KEEP OUT sign at the end of her driveway, and anyway, it wasn't exactly a driveway, just sort of a cart track, so I didn't."

Homer's interest was fired up. "Maybe I should phone her."

Joe shook his head. "Doesn't have a phone. Lives alone, never goes anywhere."

"Well, how does she survive? She must buy food somehow."

Joe shrugged. "I don't know. Maybe she lives on roots and berries like an old witch in the woods." He stood up and waved his hands in apology. "No, no, I shouldn't say such a thing. I should worry about her health, old recluse like that. I notified the Council on Seniors, but they didn't have any luck, either. I hear that the town nurse really kicked up a ruckus, but it was still no soap." Joe was scrambling into his suit coat. "Sorry, Homer, I've got to go. Church school superintendent, she's waiting for me."

"Oh, well, okay." Homer stood up, too, and grinned at Joe. "It'll be different with Miss Flint and me. I'll just turn on the old Irish charm."

Joe's "Good luck" sounded doubtful. He charged out the door, then dodged back in again, having forgotten something important. "Say, Homer, they tell me that book of yours is a bestseller." Joe strode across the room to shake Homer's hand. "Congratulations. I'm on the waiting list for it at the library."

Fat lot of good that'll do my book sales, thought Homer ungratefully as Joe rushed out again. From the far end of the corridor, Joe was shouting something else. Something about old Miss Flint? What was the word? *Gray? Hay? Play? Sleigh?*

As Homer's car headed south in the direction of Route 2A, he guessed what Joe had been shouting. It was Miss Flint's first name, Fay.

The Witch in
the Woods

A t first, Homer couldn't find the track going off into the woods, where the fabled Miss Flint was living like a witch on roots and berries. Quarry Pond Road ended at Route 2A, and from there a left turn soon brought Homer to the pizza parlor, but if there was a nearby track going off into the woods to the place where the fabled Miss Flint was living like a witch on roots and berries, he couldn't find it. As he turned the car around, a fragrance wafted past his nose and he could almost taste his favorite flavor, pepperoni with plenty of mozzarella. This time, staring left and right, he found what he was looking for. Tall weeds obscured the KEEP OUT sign, but the path was faintly visible. Homer parked the car on the shoulder of the road, pushed through the weeds, and set foot on the path.

It was a long walk up and down through a forest of white
pines, oaks and hemlocks, with here and there the gaunt trunk
of a dead tree. Homer recognized the low bushes on either side,
and he wondered if the gnarled hands of the hungry old witch
reached down to gather the blueberries. But then he came to
her vegetable garden. Well, of course old Miss Flint would have
a vegetable garden. Blueberries alone wouldn't keep an old lady
alive.

Cautiously, Homer moved closer. He saw no witch's cottage,
but as he leaned over the fence, he heard a noise and caught a
movement out of the corner of his eye, the flick of a garment, a
swaying in the tall grass. The slammed gate shivered. A rake
tipped over in a slow arc.

It was clear that the dear old lady needed time to prepare for a
visitor. She'd want to comb her witchy hair and poke the fire under the caldron. Well, no, of course there wouldn't be a caldron,
but surely there'd be a teapot. She'd want to put the kettle on.

Politely, Homer passed the time by inspecting the witch's
garden. What did poisonous plants look like? Henbane and so
on? Peering inquisitively through the chicken wire, he saw only
lettuces in a row and early peas climbing twiggy sticks, just as
they were doing at home. But this garden was far neater than
the one Mary had so carelessly planted in May. No creeping
Charlie romped among these tomato plants, no evil crabgrass
sprawled around the zucchini. Homer was envious. He told
himself that both he and Mary had more important things to do
than weed the tomato patch. They were far too busy to be nasty
neat like this, whereas a witchy old lady in the woods had nothing better to do.

He stopped inspecting the garden and wandered around it to
the gate. Here there was a path. Homer sauntered blithely along
it until he came to a low building nestled in bushy beds of
marigolds. It was not a moss-grown witch's cottage, but a clap-
boarded house as neat as the garden. The door was shut and curtains hid the windows.

Homer was an experienced old trespasser. Boldly, he knocked on the door. No one came to open it, but he could feel the presence of someone on the other side, listening. At the window, the curtains trembled. He moved to the window, tapped on the glass, and called, "Miss Flint?" in a syrupy voice, trying to sound like a courteous Visigoth, a gracious Assyrian whose descent on the fold was entirely in accordance with etiquette. He could see a shadowy form behind the gap in the curtain, but it made no move to let him in. Rashly, Homer tried a touch of cheery informality. "Fay?" he called sweetly, beaming through the gap in the curtain and pressing his nose against the glass.

At once, a thin hand reached out and slapped the curtain shut.

1868

Josiah's Ax

Measured a chestnut stump on Asa White's land, twenty-three and nine-twelfths feet in circumference, eight and one half feet one way, seven feet the other, at one foot from ground.

—Henry Thoreau, *Journal,*
June 2, 1852

A Battlefield

Josiah Gideon had been away for three days in Boston, attending a State House hearing on the cost of pauper relief and the funding of almshouses. He had prepared a fighting speech, but the mills of the legislature ground slowly.

He was the last in a long parade of interested parties, some with outrageous arguments for a reduction in spending, others good-hearted but soft-spoken. Josiah was not soft-spoken. The walls of the hearing chamber echoed with his fury, his thundered statistics, his scandalized report on conditions he had witnessed for himself. His eyes blazed, he thumped the table and shook his fist, and then he ended by reminding the legislative committee of a bitter old saying, The poor are brought up with a reverence for God, the hope of heaven, and fear of the poorhouse.

It was late afternoon when he stumbled out of the State House, made his way to the livery stable, and set out for home under a threatening sky. Before long, the heavens opened. Josiah's wife had pleaded with him to go by rail, and now he regretted his refusal. The wind became a tempest, the rain came down in sheets, and the road before him was pitch-dark. It was four o'clock in the morning when he led his horse into the stable, rubbed down her streaming sides, forked hay into her stall, felt his way into the house, pulled off his drenched coat, and climbed the stairs.

Julia lifted her head from the pillow and said, "Oh, Josiah" as he crept in beside her in his nightshirt. But after throwing one arm over her, he fell instantly asleep. Her bad news would have to wait. Julia closed her eyes and curled close to her husband, dreading the morning.

Josiah slept late. Julia went about her morning chores, tiptoeing upstairs now and then to look in the bedroom door, but Josiah slept on and on. She made breakfast for Isabelle and James. When she brought the tray into James's room, they looked at her anxiously. "Does he know yet?" said Isabelle.

Julia shook her head. Then James made a sound and looked up at the ceiling. There were footsteps overhead. Josiah was up and about. There was no putting it off. Isabelle could see the foreboding on her mother's face as Julia climbed the stairs.

"Josiah," murmured Julia, "come to the window."

"What is it?" He was buttoning his shirt, but when she said nothing, he turned to look at her, and something in her manner warned him. He crossed the room in one stride, looked out, and uttered a shout of horror. The chestnut tree was gone.

Fearfully, Julia watched him throw on the rest of his clothes. As he wrenched open the bedroom door, her hand on his sleeve meant, Gently, Josiah.

It was too late for gentleness. Across the road, the lower slope of the graveyard was a battlefield. All the mighty branches of the

chestnut tree lay tumbled and sprawling on the ground. While
he had been away, the careless axes and the long two-handled
saws of the brothers Fitzmorris had hacked and ground their
way through the living wood.

It had been the work of a single day. Yesterday morning,
Brendan and Daniel had begun the task by sharpening the steel
blades of their axes. They had carried them to the graveyard,
along with a number of saws with kerfs of different widths, a
pail of water, and a ladle. Standing under the tree, they looked
up and studied it, then walked all around it, prodding the rough
bark and choosing the place to begin. Then they hefted their
axes and began chopping. Brendan chopped cut a notch on the
north side, the side that was intended to tip and fall. Daniel's
notch was on the south, a little higher up the tree. But the heavy
work of felling was left to the sharp slanted teeth of their various saws. Patiently, the brothers sent a crosscut saw wheezing
back and forth until the weight of the tree caught and held it,
and then they pounded wedges into the notch and began again.
But not even their long two-handled saws could drive all the
way through the central core of the tree, so Brendan and Daniel
sliced off edges—east, south, and west—until the longest saw
could handle what was left.

Halfway through the work, they stopped for a dram, a chunk
of salt pork, and a slab of bread. Then both of them stretched
out flat on the grass and slept in the shade of the doomed tree,
the last kindly shade it would ever let fall. They did not sleep
long. Soon they were up and at it again, laboring steadily, hour
after hour, heaving their axes and driving their saws in and out.
About five o'clock in the afternoon, they saw a trembling thrill
run through the leaves overhead, and the tree began to creak on
its narrow stem.

From then on, it was a delicate matter of chopping and jumping back and gazing up and darting in again to strike another
blow, then jumping back and looking up again. Then at last, the
tree began to sigh and sway, and they knew the job was done.

Standing safely back out of the way, Brendan and Daniel Fitzmorris watched the triumphant conclusion of their long day's work as the vast cloudy head of leaves slowly moved against the sky, then toppled in a floundering mass. The two sawyers braced themselves, then staggered as the earth shook and the horizon quivered and the boughs thrashed from side to side. It was like watching the death throes of some majestic beast. Silently, the two brothers waited until the tree no longer throbbed and every leaf hung still.

Then, chuckling, Brendan and Daniel shook hands and climbed the hill to collect their promised fee and the preacher's thanks for a job well done. But at the door of the parsonage, they were surprised by the pallor of Preacher Biddle's face and by the trembling of his hands as he counted out their pay. No thanks were expressed for the success of their long day's work, but they were content with the cash in their pockets. Aching in every limb, they set out for home, ducking their heads as the rain came down.

The next day was Sunday, a fine bright morning after the violent storm of the night before. The sky was clear and sparkling as Josiah Gideon stumbled across the road to look at the wreckage. All that remained standing of the ancient trunk was a vast stump, like a vulgar joke. Sick at heart, he waded through the leafy tangle, bending to stroke the flat furrows of the bark or break off a spray of leaves. Before long, his grief was transformed into anger, and his anger into a powerful resolution, a new and wild idea.

Catching Prayers

It was the Sabbath. Julia dressed for church in a house that steamed with the delirium of Josiah's unspoken wrath. As she pulled on her gloves she could hear the rumbling wheeze of his grindstone. Looking back from the gate, she saw her husband crouched over the revolving stone, his right foot violently working the treadle, his ax blade glittering in the morning sun.

It was a balmy morning. Jack and Jacob Spratt, those celebrated portrait and aerial photographers, were making good on the aerial part of their promise. The balloon tugged at the guy ropes and nodded over their heads as they lifted the camera into the basket. It was mounted on a contraption invented by Jake, a cantilevered arm that suspended it over the side.

Today, they had a plan. Wherever the wind might carry them,

they would take panoramic views of main streets and town squares, mercantile establishments and church steeples, houses and barns. Later on, Jake would print handsome images from the exposed plates to astonish prominent citizens, mayors, city councillors, and village selectmen.

The splendid prints would be offered at prices tenderly quoted by Jack, who had an inborn gift of gab. "Well, I don't know," a selectman might say, but they knew how his eyes would bulge at the unfamiliar views of his native town, and sooner or later he would surely persuade the rest of the board to come up with the price. And as likely as not, he would pluck Jack's sleeve and ask for a private sitting. "Just me and the wife? And maybe my shop with the clerks outside in a row?"

So it promised to be a profitable venture.

This morning, Hector was ready to follow along. He had tossed a sack of oats into his wagon, greased the wheels, and whispered encouragement to his old nag. Now he licked his finger and held it up to the gentle breeze. "Wind's just right," he said. "West-nor'west."

It was the last Sunday in June. The balloon lifted softly and drifted over green fields and wooded hills. Jack handed the plate holders to his brother, and Jake tipped the camera to capture two Lincoln churches and a town hall. Then he eased it a little to the right to record the center of Concord, where their mobile studio had done such a land-office business a few weeks back.

"Hear the bell, Jake?" said Jack. "See all them people going into that there church?"

Jake laughed. "Bell's going up and down on the wheel, Jack. See that?"

Jack laughed, too, and once again they had the proud sense of being citizens of the air, angelic visitants looking down on the earthbound creatures below.

Churchgoing faces looked up. Loungers on the Milldam looked up. As they drifted over the road to Barrett's mill, a small boy looked up and clapped his hands. His grandmother looked up, too, and waved her handkerchief.

Then Jack gripped the rim of the basket and Jake clung to the camera as the balloon began to wallow. The wind had changed. Cupping his hands beside his mouth, Jack hollered down to Hector, "You all right, Hector?"

Standing up in the wagon as it hurtled after them along the road to Nashoba, Hector had no breath to shout back. His horse was laboring and foaming at the mouth. Hector flicked the whip, but only in show. The poor old plug, she couldn't go no faster.

In the basket floating high over Hector's head, Jake heaped more coal on the fire and the balloon lifted slightly, carrying them over a Concord orchard and a Nashoba field of sprouting corn. Jack handed Jake another plate and Jake readied the camera. The small domed steeple of the church was rising above the trees. Then the burial ground came in sight.

"Mercy," said Jake, "will you look at that there stump."

"Where at, Jake?" said Jack.

"Down there in the graveyard." Jake aimed the camera and squeezed the bulb. "Remember that big tree?" Then he snatched out the plate holder, installed another plate, and swiveled the cantilever to photograph the church.

"Mighty quiet down there, Jake," said Jack. "Can't hear no singing."

"Praying, that's what they're doing, Jack. All them people, they're down on their knees saying their prayers."

"Might catch a few on the way up, Jake." Jokingly, Jack held out his hand as if to catch a flying prayer.

But in the sanctuary of the church, below the drifting balloon, most of the silent appeals of the Nashoba congregation were merely bursts of feeling, too ephemeral to be caught in an outstretched hand. Some were wordless explosions of sorrow. On the way into the church for the morning service, everyone had seen the devastation in the burying ground. There had been horrified stares at the fallen tree and shocked exclamations of dismay.

"Reverend Gideon, he ordered it," whispered a parishioner who had witnessed the murder. "You hear that?" whispered another. "Parson did it." In the pews, there were murmurs of anger and grief.

Ella Viles had no particular interest in the fate of the chestnut tree. In the pew where she sat with lowered head between her mother and father, she was envisioning her wedding. She could see it as clearly as if it were actually happening—her slow progress up the aisle, her silk train reaching far back over the carpet, her veil floating behind her as she moved toward the pulpit, where Eben Flint stood waiting. Eben's face was dim. She saw only her wedding dress. Dreamily, she added lace insertions to the bodice, a chemisette and a quilling of ribbon around the sleeves.

In the pew behind Ella Viles sat Julia Gideon. Julia's prayer was true and fervent, but, as always, it was pointless. What could she pray for, after all? Not for the restoration of James Shaw's handsome face, nor the sight of his left eye, nor the return of his two hands. For what, then? Julia's head bowed lower. Only for the courage to bear it, for James, for Isabelle, and for herself. Then, clasping her gloved hands tighter in her lap, Julia prayed for her husband. Josiah's anger alarmed her.

As for the prayer of the Reverend Horatio Biddle, it was a wild jumble. With his face buried in his hands, Horatio tried to persuade the Almighty that the destruction of the finest tree in the county of Middlesex had been a pious act, rather than an error of judgment.

The prayer of his wife was not confused at all. It was direct and articulate. If the brothers Spratt could have caught her prayer as it shot skyward through the roof of the church and streaked past the balloon, they might have pursed their lips and tut-tutted, because Ingeborg's prayer to the Supreme Being was more in the nature of a curse upon the head of her husband's enemy, the Reverend Josiah Gideon.

But then in a single instant, all the prayers in the sanctuary of the First Parish Church of Nashoba, whether addressed to the God of Abraham or to the editor of *Godey's Lady's Book* or to the Devil himself, were interrupted by a crash from the burial ground.

Julia winced and looked up. Could that terrible noise be the sound of Josiah's ax?

The Lift and Fall
of the Ax

The service came to a close much earlier than usual. Horatio Biddle's sermon ended with a "thirdly" rather than a "tenthly." At every crash from the burial ground, Horatio flinched and the face of his wife grew darker. When he quavered, "We will forego the final hymn," there was a slamming shut of hymnbooks and a rush for the door.

The noonday sun shone brightly down on the green hillside, on the scattered tombstones and the pale stump of the chestnut tree. It shone on the strange spectacle of Josiah Gideon savagely at work in the welter of fallen branches, and on the men and women flooding out of the church to watch the lift and fall of his ax. It shone on the woman who came last, picking her way slowly among the gravestones, Julia Gideon.

Ingeborg Biddle followed, too, in an equal state of dismay. Her husband strode ahead of her, trying to persuade himself that it had been Josiah Gideon who had committed the original offense by desecrating the resting place of Deacon Sweetser. "Sir," he shouted at Josiah, "may I ask what you think you are doing?"

Josiah gave him a burning glance, steadied a thick bough under his foot, lifted the ax, and brought it whistling down.

"Church property," cried Horatio. "I command you, sir, to desist."

Josiah did not desist. *Crash* went his ax, and *crash* again.

Courageously, Horatio Biddle took a step forward, as though to wrest the ax from the madman's hands, but when Josiah turned toward him with the ax held high, Horatio thought better of it and withdrew. Ingeborg withdrew also. As she stumbled away, she stared straight into the faces of her friends for sympathy, but Elfrida Poole looked down, and Ella Viles simpered, and Abigail Whittey blew her nose. Only Julia Gideon gave Ingeborg a direct and troubled glance.

Thirty-seven men and women of the congregation remained in a silent circle around the prostrate tree, watching the powerful lift and crashing fall of Josiah Gideon's ax. If any precise recorder had been on hand to note down the names, his list would have looked like this:

Arthur Wall, pharmacist
Frank Wheeler, attorney, and **Martha Wheeler**
George Blood, farmer, and his wife, **Pearl**
Elfrida Poole, widow, mistress of the pianoforte
Samuel Bigelow, judge of the district court, and **Lydia Bigelow,**
    arranger of noonings, fairs, and bake sales for the benefit of the
    parish
Phineas Wilder, postmaster, and **Wilhelmina Wilder**
Jarvis Brown, attorney, and **Eliza Brown**
David Kibbee, dairy farmer and selectman

Potter Viles, merchant, his wife, **Joan,** and daughter, **Ella**
The Misses **Dorothea** and **Margaret Rochester**
Miss **Abigail Whittey,** widow
Jedediah Eaton, professor of Latin at Harvard College
Samuel Brooks, retired clergyman
Joseph Hunt, farmer, and **Eugenia Hunt,** painter of artistic lamp
    shades
David Monroe, farmer, and his widowed mother, **Alice**
Jonas Todd, banker, and **Dorothea Todd**
Theodore Wilbur, district schoolmaster
Charles Holland, farmer, and **Annie Holland**
Artemus Grout, sheriff, and **Eleanora Grout**
Reuben Mills, farmer, and **Dora Mills**
Miss **Cynthia Smith,** spinster
Douglas Pease, merchant
Richard Doll, resident, **Nashoba Home Farm**

Gradually, the crowd thinned and dispersed, until no one was
left but Josiah, savagely rending branches from the trunk of the
tree. But within the hour, Ted Wilbur was back with an armful
of tools, and by evening the whole town of Nashoba echoed
with the crashing of axes and the wheezing of crosscut saws.

Women and children had come, too, and now, following the
sturdy example of Lydia Bigelow, they were stumbling in the
tumbled chaos of the shattered tree, hauling away the heavy
boughs and dragging them into piles.

Julia Gideon was not among them. Julia was at home, watching from the window of the sitting room, not knowing whether
to be glad or sorry. The gathering of carts and buggies and the
cheerful confusion were exhilarating, but at the same time she
was profoundly distressed by her husband's fury. No matter how
righteous it was, no matter how justified, where would it lead
him? Unable to watch any longer or listen to the buzzing of the
saws and the chopping whack of the axes, Julia withdrew to the

kitchen and made noises of her own, thumping bowls on the table and clashing her bread pans.

At another window, James kept his own vigil. When Isabelle said, "James, would you like to lie down?" he shook his head violently. Resigned, she left him and joined her mother in the kitchen. The fire in the stove had gone out. Isabelle lifted the lid of the firebox, dropped in a bundle of kindling, and set it alight.

James remained alone at his window, watching the turmoil across the road. In anguish, he thought of the use he could make of the hooks on his arms if only he could be out there with the others. His strong arms quivered in their eagerness to grasp and haul away the heaviest of the severed branches.

When Isabelle heard a knock on the door, she ran to throw it open for Eben Flint. There was no need to speak. Eben looked at her soberly and went at once to James. Eagerly, James turned from the window and lifted his hooked hands. Eben understood him at once, but he only gripped James by the shoulder and left the house with a whetstone in one hand and an ax in the other. Soon he was over the wall and hard at work with the others, slashing at the limbs of the fallen tree.

From the top of the burial ground, high on the knoll beside the church, the tall stone of Deacon Sweetser looked serenely down.

Advice from
Julius Caesar

Professor Jedediah Eaton

The steam-powered sawmill stood directly below Quarry Pond Road, kitty-corner to the house of Josiah Gideon. Isaac Pole, the sawyer, stood in his cluttered yard, looking up at the commotion across the way. He yelled at Eben Flint, "You got to open up that stone wall."

Eben shouted, "I know." He dropped his ax and threw himself at the task, picking up lichen-covered stones and thumping them down a dozen yards away.

"What about those very large boulders down there at the bottom?" said Professor Eaton, coming up to assess the situation and offer scholarly advice. Surely Julius Caesar had run across obstacles of this nature during the Gallic Wars.

"Oh, we'll think of something," said Eben, staggering under

the weight of two heavy stones, and then Josiah Gideon lowered his ax long enough to shout, "Crowbars, Eben. You'll find two in my shed, maybe three."

Professor Eaton followed Eben around the corner and into Josiah's shed, explaining along the way the astonishing achievements of Caesar during his conquest of Gaul. "For example, Mr. Flint, his towering siege engines. Caesar's legions rolled them right up to the enemy's very walls." And while Eben poked in dark corners in Josiah's shed, looking for crowbars and cant hooks, Professor Eaton discoursed on the foolish belief of the Belgians that the Romans had accomplished this feat with divine aid, when of course it had been their superb engineering skill. "Surely, Mr. Flint," urged the professor as Eben started back up the road, "Roman ingenuity might be called upon in the present crisis."

"Why, yes, how extremely interesting, professor," said Eben, lugging heavy tools in one hand and dragging a stoneboat with the other.

"I'll take one of those crows," said David Kibbee, the dairy farmer, whose fourteen cows kept many a local family supplied with butter and milk. Artemus Grout helped himself to another. Soon both of them were hard at work, helping Eben pry massive boulders out of the ground while Professor Eaton delivered a lecture on the construction of Roman bridges.

The afternoon sun was warm. By the middle of the afternoon, the heavy work was done. The fallen trunk of the chestnut tree lay bare and shorn of its limbs, and the opening in the stone wall gaped thirty feet wide.

The axmen put down their tools. Eben collapsed on the ground, and so did David and Artemus. The women's work was finished, too, and they laughed at one another's straggling hair. Satisfied and exhausted, the men and women of the congregation gathered up their tools and set off for home. Only Professor Eaton, Josiah Gideon, and Eben Flint remained behind.

Professor Eaton had stopped lecturing, but now he picked up

a cobblestone and carried it to the rock pile as a symbolic gesture of support. Eben smiled and said, "We certainly thank you for your help, professor."

"Oh, no, don't thank me." Professor Eaton dusted his coattails, quoted Catullus—"*Noli admirari,* after all"—and said good-bye.

"Sir," said Eben to Josiah, "I expect you must be pretty tired."

"Tired!" Josiah's shirt was dark with sweat, his face was scoured with scratches, there were blisters on the palms of his hands, and the tip of his left thumb bled from a grazing blow of the ax, but he was in a transport. "No, no," cried Josiah, "I'm fresh as the morning."

From across the road, the sawyer shouted. "I'm getting up a head of steam. Why don't you gentlemen trundle me down a few of them there logs?"

The Sawmill

Isaac Pole stood in a calculating posture beside a heap of lopped branches in the graveyard. "This one will do easy," he said, bending over the thickest log and spanning it with his hand.

"It's very good of you, Isaac," said Josiah, "to get up steam on a Sunday."

"Sabbath don't mean nothing to me," said Isaac, opening the jaw of his peavey.

"As a matter of fact," said Josiah, "it's a good thing it happens to be a Sunday. Any other day of the week, all those good people would have been someplace else."

Eben grinned. "And what would we have done without Professor Eaton?"

"Big strong fella?" said Isaac.

"Pretty strong on advice," said Eben. He set his hands on one end of the heavy branch and braced himself.

"Straight from Julius Caesar," said Josiah, spreading his hands on the other end.

Isaac gripped the middle of the log with the peavey and together they tried to shove it toward the gap in the wall. It wobbled and began to roll. Isaac pulled the peavey loose and ran after the log as it slid neatly through the gap in the wall, rolled across the slant of Quarry Pond Road, bounced across his yard, tumbled through the open front of the sawmill, and thudded to a stop on the log carriage. "There she is, nice and easy," shouted Isaac above the hiss of the steam and the thump of the engine. At once, he slammed down the iron dogs to hold the log in place and fiddled with the setting to adjust the width of the first cut.

The mill was hot with steam. Isaac ran around, disappearing behind clouds of vapor, appearing again to adjust his belts and pulleys. The arms of the governor flew sideways, the flywheel turned, the shavings in the firebox blazed, the boiler sent hot steam into the pipe, and a whizzing belt turned the arbor of the great round saw.

By midafternoon, a pile of newly cut boards lay at the foot of the slanting ways. "What you mean to do with these here boards?" shouted Isaac, chucking another one off to the side. The board slid down the ways and thunked into the pile and bounced and settled. The engine roared and steam puffed out of the boiler.

"It depends," said Josiah. He helped Isaac roll another log in place on the carriage. "How many board feet have we got, do you guess? I mean altogether."

Isaac spiked the log into place with the iron dogs and thought it over. "Six thousand," he said at last, "maybe seven." He pulled the lever to start the carriage moving, a belt whizzed, wheels turned, and the log moved forward.

Josiah shook his head and yelled, "Not enough."

Isaac jerked out the dogs, tumbled the log a quarter turn,

spiked it again, and sent it forward into the saw. Glancing keenly at Josiah as the blade stripped off another piece of bark, he bawled, "Rumor has it you mean to build some kind of sacred edifice."

"Who told you that?"

"My wife," hollered Isaac. He grinned and yelled something about wifely tittle-tattle, but it was lost in the scream of the saw.

One by one, during the rest of that long afternoon and throughout all the following day, the branches of the chestnut tree were milled into boards. The saw shrieked through rough bark and clean wood. Isaac was everywhere at once, oiling the moving parts or pumping water into the boiler, or feeding the fire, or jerking back on the feed handle to send a log forward into the teeth of the saw, or shoving the handle forward to back it up and begin a new cut. His clothes were singed and his hands and face were black with grease, but his small sharp eyes missed nothing.

There was a crisis on Monday morning when one of the skids cracked and sagged under the weight of a heavy log. The log had to be lifted and rolled out of the way and the broken skid replaced. Isaac heaved and cursed. Josiah heaved and gasped.

By four o'clock on Monday afternoon, nothing was left in the burial ground but a jumble of chopped twigs, heaps of sawdust, and the dismembered trunk of the tree.

Josiah and Isaac stood side by side, looking down at the enormous carcass from which a hundred thick limbs had been cut away, and Josiah said, "I don't suppose, Isaac, you could handle anything this big across?"

"Got a system," said Isaac proudly. "You get this here log into my mill, Josiah Gideon, and I swear to God I'll cut it up."

It took a yoke of oxen to accomplish Josiah's part of the bargain. Straining forward, the matched pair dragged the chained trunk of the chestnut tree through the gap in the stone wall and across the road. When the massive log was at last hauled up the skids onto the carriage of Isaac's sawmill, cant-hooked in place and bulking so high above the teeth of the saw that it grazed the rafters, Isaac prodded it, gazed at it, and pranced around it. Milling it into boards would be the greatest work of his life.

After shouting for two days, he had no voice left. His thinning hair was powdered with sawdust and his eyes burned red in his blackened face, but Isaac grinned at Josiah and spat on his hands.

At home, Josiah whirled his arms and made slicing gestures to illustrate Isaac's heroic system of milling the massive trunk of the chestnut tree. "He ran that log past the saw and cut off a small piece from one side, and then he canted it a few degrees and ran it through again. He just went on around and around, cutting slices from the edge, anyplace the saw could reach, until that prodigious log was small enough to handle."

Julia lifted her hands in wonder, Isabelle said, "What a miracle," and James nodded and bowed his head.

While these turbulent events were happening in the burying ground and across the road in the sawmill of Isaac Pole, life in the parsonage of Horatio and Ingeborg Biddle was in a state of crisis.

All Sunday afternoon, Horatio watched from the kitchen window, observing the alarming scene at the bottom of the hill. Dozens of his own parishioners were at work around the fallen tree, chopping and sawing and dragging branches into piles. Squinting between the curtains, he quailed. Could that bearded man in shirtsleeves be Samuel Bigelow, chairman of the Prudential Committee? With dread in his heart, Horatio watched as the stone wall was torn apart and heavy branches rolled across the road into the sawmill of that notoriously unchurched citizen of Nashoba, Isaac Pole.

While Horatio maintained his post at the window, Ingeborg bustled around the kitchen as if she had not a care in the world.

She whacked at a slab of bacon with a cleaver and whipped up eggs in a bowl. But before long, she was huddled at the window beside her husband, peering through an opera glass. "Horatio," she murmured, "we must go to law."

"What? Go to law!"

"That man is purloining the property of this church. He should be prosecuted for criminal trespass and grand larceny. And, Horatio, just think of his first offense." Ingeborg put down the opera glass and looked at her husband in triumph. "What could be more illegal than robbing a grave?"

Horatio made an uncertain noise in his throat and looked down again at the scene in the burial ground. Where there had once been a massive tree, he now had an unobstructed view of the property across the Acton Turnpike, the home of Josiah Gideon.

NOW

Carlisle Steeples

Tablecloths—HELP!

Scandals
and Skateboards

First Religious Society, Carlisle

I'm sick of it," said Homer as they locked the door and trudged down the porch steps.

"Sick of what?"

"The past. Ancient ladies decaying in the woods and all this groping around among the bones of the dead. Why don't they just lie there and shut up? They've had their day in the sun. It's our turn now. Life's too short! Why don't we live a little?"

"Well, what would you rather do?" said Mary heartlessly. "Take off for Las Vegas?"

"Well, no, that's the whole trouble. I've lost the knack of wasting time and having fun." Homer flung open the car door and climbed in behind the wheel. "It's my doom, pursuing this foolish steeple chase to—what's the next one called?"

"Carlisle." Mary consulted her notes. "The First Religious Society of Carlisle."

The old village of Carlisle lay northeast of Nashoba and directly north of Concord. The church stood high and handsome in the center of town. Homer parked across the street, and for a moment they sat staring up at the sunlit facade. It was a beauty.

"James Gibbs," murmured Homer.

"Of course," said Mary, because it was true. Faintly echoed in the design of the First Religious Society of Carlisle they could recognize the church of St. Martin's in the Fields in Trafalgar Square. This small but elegant American building, fashioned from wooden posts and beams like a barn, was surely the remote descendant of the handsome steepled churches that had been hurried into being by Christopher Wren and James Gibbs after the great fire of London. This pretty building had no grand portico of Corinthian columns, but, like St. Martin's in the Fields, its little tower boasted the same diminishing layers, the same Grecian pediment, clock, bell chamber, and steeple pointing skyward.

"I wonder if they knew it," said Mary.

"Knew what?"

"The carpenters. I wonder if they knew their own architectural ancestry."

"It doesn't matter. They knew how to put up a sturdy building, and they had pattern books to copy."

Mary mumbled the name of Asher Benjamin as they lifted the latch of the central door and walked into the vestry. From here, a stairway led up to the sanctuary on the second floor, but they were halted at once by the notices on the bulletin board. Addicted to print, they stopped to look.

TABLECLOTHS—*HELP!*
If you have taken tablecloths home to wash after the Easter luncheon,
please return as soon as possible.

GENERAL ASSEMBLY OF THE UNITARIAN UNIVERSALIST ASSOCIATION
Sign up for workshops!
Growth Resources for Small Congregations
Wakening the Mind, Opening the Heart
Embracing Life with the Heart of a Buddha

RIDE FOR HUNGER SUNDAY, JUNE 15
Join the bicycle tour for Project Bread!

For a moment, they were mesmerized by this glimpse into the stomach, heart, and muscle of a busy congregation. Then Mary said, "Never mind," and they turned to climb the stairs.

Homer counted the steps as he gasped his way to the top. "Eighteen of them. No mercy on us old folks. Hey, will you look at that."

It was a bell rope, dangling from a hole in the ceiling of the narrow corridor at the top of the stairs. Impulsively, Homer reached out and gave it a jerk.

Mary cried, "Homer, for heaven's sake" as a loud jangle sounded from above. It was followed by a shriek from the sanctuary and a rush of pattering feet. "Now you're in for it," said Mary.

A little woman burst out of a door and cried, "May I ask what you think you are doing?"

Mary felt no pity, but Homer blushed. "Oh, I'm terribly sorry, ma'am. I only touched the rope. I didn't expect it to ring."

It was a lie, and they all knew it, but the woman's face softened—the two tall strangers looked so extremely respectable. "May I help you? My name's Milly Smith. I'm the choir director."

"We're Homer and Mary Kelly," said Mary, nodding and smiling. "We're just so interested in the history of your church."

Homer smiled and nodded, too. "We're just sort of looking into all the churches around here. Their histories, I mean."

Milly Smith narrowed her eyes and stared at Homer. "You're not the Homer Kelly who wrote that bestselling book?"

Homer beamed. "Well, yes, that's me. How did you like it?" "Oh, I haven't read it yet," said Milly. "But of course I will, any day now. How delightful. Do come in and sit down." Joyfully, she led them into the sanctuary, straight up the aisle to the pulpit and the low platform of the choir loft, where she sat them down on a bench beside the organ. At once, she began reciting the entire history of the First Religious Society of Carlisle. It was obviously her passion.

But to Homer's disappointment, there was only one scandal in the history of the church, and it was the same one that had happened everywhere: the split in the congregation at the time of the Unitarian heresy. The stalwart orthodox Congregationalists of Carlisle had walked out in the year 1829, leaving the building to the upstart Unitarians.

"I'll show you," said Milly Smith as they stood up at last, faint with hunger. "The Congregationalists built a new church right across the street."

Descending the stairs, they could hear a wild clattering from outdoors. Kids on skateboards were plunging back and forth on the paved street in front of the church, executing heroic leaps and acrobatic turns. Milly dodged around them, followed by Homer and Mary, and they stood safely out of the way, staring across the road.

Yes, there it was, another building with a steeple, a charming Victorian structure set in a green lawn. Along one side ran a row of churchlike pointed windows, but no proud sign stood beside the road, only a mailbox.

"It's been turned into offices downstairs, you see," explained Milly, "and upstairs it's a private house. The church was desanctified and sold in 1970. There's a fine new building just up the road."

"Well, thank you, Milly Smith," said Mary.

"Yes, thank you very much," added Homer. "Oh, Milly, I don't suppose you know anything about—well, I know it sounds silly—a lost church?"

"A lost church?" Milly shook her head.

"Or anything about a tree? I mean some tree or other, way back when. Or any connection with Oliver Wendell Holmes?"

"You mean Justice Holmes?" Milly looked bewildered.

"No, no, the other Holmes." Homer felt ridiculous. "The poet, the one who—"

"Come on, Homer," said Mary, tugging at his sleeve.

"I mean Dr. Holmes, the father of the justice, the Oliver Wendell Holmes who wrote *The Autocrat of the Breakfast Table.* You must have heard of that? And a lot of poems and so forth? You know who I mean?"

"Well, I guess so," said Milly Smith. "But I don't think Dr. Holmes ever worshiped in Carlisle."

Whoopsie

They were ravenous. Homer Kelly was six and a half feet tall and a trifle overweight. Without a regular succession of breakfast, morning snack, coffee break, lunch, afternoon snack, tea, happy hour, supper, and a final bedtime bowl of cereal, his legs went limp. "Hey," said Homer, zooming the car around and heading south, "there's a pizza place in Nashoba, right there on Route Two A, next to the witchy lady's place."

"Great," said Mary. "I could eat a hymnbook."

"Watch it," said Homer. "Some of those hymns might be hard to get down—"Rock of Ages" for instance."

"Ouch." Mary clutched her neck and then said firmly, "What I want is a hymn in the shape of a nice juicy pepperoni pizza with mozzarella. Hurry up, Homer."

Route 2A was a long, winding state highway. In East Cambridge and Arlington, it was known as Massachusetts Avenue; in Lexington, Marratt Road; and in Lincoln, North Great Road. In Concord, it had several names—Lexington Street, Elm Street, and finally Nashoba Road. In the towns of Nashoba and Acton, it was a suburban strip, a narrow scar through abandoned farms. Dignified old houses had been turned into furniture emporiums. Car dealerships were surrounded by glittering wreaths of Toyotas and Chevys, and beside the parking lot of an upmarket mall, trendy outlets stood cheek-to-cheek—Staples, Trader Joe's, Pier 1.

The pizza parlor in Nashoba was neither trendy nor upmarket. It fronted directly on the highway, and in the window the looped letters of an old-fashioned neon sign spelled **Nashoba Pizza.**

Homer pulled up beside a motorcycle in the weedy parking lot at the side, and Mary said, "It looks just right."

Indoors, the place was like an old-fashioned diner, complete with a long counter and twirly stools. There was even a jukebox glittering with plastic made to look like mother-of-pearl. The jukebox was howling and thumping with some kind of pop music, but Homer and Mary were too hungry to care. They sat down on the stools and waited to be noticed by the girl at the counter, who was deep in whispered conversation with a muscular kid in a pink tank top, obviously the owner of the motorcycle. The girl showed no interest in her new customers.

Mary and Homer contented themselves with choosing from the pizza list tacked to a fancy board on the wall. Then they looked expectantly at the waitress, but she was still nose-to-nose with the motorcycle guy. Homer's stomach clapped against his backbone, but he diverted himself by studying the pictures on the wall, a display of faded photographs tacked up between the list of pizzas and a large sign proclaiming NO REST ROOMS. One of the photographs showed a family standing beside a Tin Lizzie, mamma with bobbed hair, papa with cigar, two identical little boys in knickers, two identical little girls with bows in their hair.

Without warning, the music stopped. Pink Tank Top departed, and the waitress moved languidly down the counter, staring out the window at the motorcycle as it zoomed onto the highway with huge blats of its exhaust.

Mary and Homer ordered coffee and mozzarella pizzas and watched the girl unwrap two frozen objects and slap them in a microwave. Cars zoomed past on the highway, and then a rumbling procession of dump trucks. The rickety building trembled, and one of the pictures fell with a crash.

"Whoopsie," said the girl, stooping to pick it up.

Homer had caught a glimpse of the picture as it fell, and he said, "Oh, please, may we look?"

"Well, I don't give a damn." Sulkily, the bitchy girl jerked their pizzas out of the microwave, slid them onto paper plates, dumped them on the counter, then slapped the picture down beside them.

Eagerly, Homer and Mary leaned over the old brown photograph. It was a faded image of a half-inflated hot-air balloon. Two young men in bowler hats stood beside it, their arms akimbo. Charmed, Mary asked the waitress, "Do you know who they are?"

"Don't ask me." The bitchy girl was too listless to hang the picture back on its nail. Instead, she leaned it against a squeeze bottle of mustard on a tiny shelf attached to an elaborate cupboard.

But there were many more pictures on the wall. Homer was delighted. He pointed excitedly left and right. "Maybe they show what old Nashoba was like. What about that one? Oh, please, might we see that one?"

"Watch it, Homer," cried Mary, but she was too late. Homer's sweeping gesture had knocked over his coffee cup.

"Whoopsie," said the bitchy girl again, mopping up the slop.

1868

The Autocrat of the Breakfast Table

> . . . *I have a most intense, passionate fondness for trees in general, and have had several romantic attachments to certain trees in particular.*

> —Oliver Wendell Holmes, *The Autocrat of the Breakfast Table*

A Favorite of
Dr. Holmes

I n the bedchamber just down the hall from the bathroom that
was so splendidly appointed with fixtures from the J. L. Mott
Iron Works in New York City, Horatio Biddle could not sleep.
He turned and tossed. Visions of Josiah Gideon and Samuel
Bigelow tumbled in his head, and also the shocking sight of a favorite teacher in the Sabbath school snipping at twigs with her
embroidery scissors. Professor Jedediah Eaton had not been snipping or chopping, but his very presence with the others had been
a blow. Horatio pulled the pillow over his head, but he couldn't
banish the memory of Professor Eaton's shiny spectacles, his scholarly whiskers, and the opening and shutting of his faraway mouth.

These nightmarish images were bad enough, but at two
o'clock in the morning, Horatio reared up in bed as another
thought occurred to him, and it was far more horrible.

Slipping out of bed, careful not to awaken his wife, Horatio crept downstairs in the dark. In his study, he lighted the lamp with trembling fingers, carried it to the bookcase, and moved it along a shelf until he found what he was looking for, *The Autocrat of the Breakfast Table,* by Oliver Wendell Holmes.

Horatio set the lamp down on his desk beside the bust of Cicero, then leafed through the book, his heart thudding in his breast. Yes, here was the passage he remembered. Dr. Holmes was rambling on and on about his "tree-wives," the great trees that were his special delight, the old giants he loved to measure with his thirty-foot tape: ". . . I shall speak of trees as we see them, love them, adore them in the fields, where they are alive, holding their green sun-shades over our heads, talking to us with their hundred thousand whispering tongues . . ."

Nervously, Horatio turned page after page as the autocrat harangued the breakfast table on the subject of great trees. Paragraph after paragraph was devoted to his favorites, the Johnston elm, the vast elms of Springfield, Northampton, and Hatfield, and, good God, here was an alarming story about a tall poplar that had been criminally cut down.

And then Horatio's lifeless fingers nearly dropped the book as he came upon the paragraph he had half-remembered:

> Now let us glory in the great *Castanea dentata* that stands in the burial ground in the town of Nashoba. This magnificent chestnut tree is a monument to our national history, a survivor from the seventeenth century, when it began life before the village itself existed, when few settlers dwelt beyond the limits of the town of Concord. Who knows but that deep within its mighty heart lies buried an arrow shot from the bow of a Nashoba warrior, the last of the tribe of Nipmucks who claimed these woods as their native soil?

Horatio closed the book, put it back on the shelf, and extinguished the lamp. Crawling back into bed beside his sleeping wife, he vowed never to reveal to her this painful news. At the same time, he prayed earnestly that Dr. Holmes might never again set foot in Nashoba to pay his respects to that "monument to our national history," the magnificent chestnut tree in the burial ground, now cut down, destroyed, and vanished forever at the whim of Horatio Theophilus Biddle.

Ingeborg Goes to Law

It was infuriating to Ingeborg Biddle that her husband refused to take up the matter. What on earth possessed him? The case was perfectly clear. Josiah Gideon had violated an ancient grave and stolen valuable property belonging to the church. Justice demanded that he be prosecuted.

Well, if Horatio lacked the backbone to go to law, Ingeborg did not. She could not forget the humiliation of her outhouse encounter with Josiah Gideon. She was determined to seek revenge. Next day, she prepared herself for a visit to the office of attorney Jarvis Brown by dressing with care in a new outfit, one that required a different sort of undergirding. The wide-spreading skirts that had been popular during the war were no longer in style. Postwar fashion called for a more slender silhouette that billowed out at the back.

Ingeborg was a fleshy woman, but she pulled tight the strings of her stays and adjusted the new contraption around her waist. Then she hooked, snapped, and buttoned herself into her new gown, stepped out the door, and walked past the town green to the offices of Peabody and Brown. Of course, the name of the firm no longer meant an actual partnership, since Moses Peabody had passed away long ago. Stalwartly, Ingeborg mounted the stairs, eased her skirts into a chair, and explained to Mr. Brown the case against Josiah Gideon.

"I see," said Mr. Brown, although he was already acquainted with the matter. By word of mouth, news of the extraordinary events of the previous day had raced all over town. "This concerns an unauthorized reinterment in the graveyard as well as the removal of valuable timber, is that correct?"

"Exactly." Ingeborg edged forward on the chair. She was not yet used to the apparatus around her waist, and the bunched fabric took up so much room, she was afraid of slipping onto the floor.

If she expected Mr. Brown to seize his pen and begin scribbling a document couched in Olympian language, a lawsuit against that plundering bandit Josiah Gideon, she was disappointed.

"The burial ground belongs to the church?" asked Mr. Brown mildly. "Are you completely certain?" And then he posed several other thorny questions: Did any interments in the burial ground antedate the founding of the church? Had every person interred on the premises been a professing Christian? Had every one of them belonged to the congregation of the Nashoba Parish Church? Had it occurred to Mrs. Biddle that the burial ground might actually be the property of the town itself, a secular body established by the action of the Great and General Court of Massachusetts?

Taken aback, Ingeborg protested that although she did not actually know the facts in the case, it was common knowledge that the burial ground belonged to the church.

Mr. Brown merely looked at her serenely and advised her to look into the matter. "If it can in fact be proved," he said, rising to show her to the door, "that the ground on which the tree stood was indeed the property of the church, then I will be most happy to write up a suit of wrongful seizure against the Reverend Josiah Gideon. Good day to you, Mrs. Biddle."

Outdoors again in the harsh light of noonday, Ingeborg set off a little uncertainly for home. The street resounded with the rumble of farmers' carts and the rattle of buggy wheels, but overwhelming everything else was a wild scream from the sawmill of Isaac Pole as the savage iron teeth of his steam-driven saw tore into the wood of the chestnut tree, transforming the logs into boards that were rightfully the property of Nashoba's First Parish Church and its pastor, the Reverend Horatio Biddle.

Program Chairman

Eben Flint was a resident of the town of Concord, not Nashoba. But when the program chairman of the Nashoba Lyceum retired, Potter Viles paid a call on Eben to ask him to fill the vacancy.

No doubt the request was urged on Mr. Viles by his daughter, Ella. At any rate, Ella insisted on driving her father to the Flint homestead in the Jenny Lind. As she halted the horse in front of the house, loud music poured from the window of the sitting room, where Eben's mother was rollicking through a favorite hymn and accompanying herself on the organ.

"O Lamb of God," sang Eudocia, but she stopped abruptly when Eben shot past her to open the door.

"To tell you the truth, Mr. Flint," said Potter Viles, settled on the sofa, "our committee has exhausted all the possibilities for speakers that we can think of."

"And we can't bother dear Mr. Emerson again," said Ella. "He has already favored us twice."

Eben was flattered. "Well, I could try my hand. We might go a little farther afield. I'll see what I can do."

By suppertime, he had decided where to start. He left the rest of the family discussing the subject of public speaking and went upstairs to his room to write a letter.

Around the table, the suggestions were plentiful. Even Sallie made a critical remark: "Why does the speaker always have to be a man? Why not a woman?"

"Good for you, Sallie," said Ida.

"Second the motion," cried Eudocia.

But Alexander only laughed. "The Concord Lyceum had a woman last year, remember, Mother Flint? She wasn't very good, but it was amazing she could do it at all."

"Alexander!" Ida was indignant.

"My dear, I was only joking. I'm sure you could do a better job yourself."

"Not better, perhaps," said Ida, "but I could certainly do it." She smiled around the table. "What would I lecture about?"

"I have it," said Alexander. " 'Mrs. Alexander Clock will present a discourse on how to be an obedient and dutiful wife.' "

"No, no." Ida gathered her skirts and climbed up on her chair. "Ladies and gentlemen," she said, waving her arms in elocutionary gestures, "for all those of you with ears to hear, I will now explain how to organize a harvest festival. I assure you, ladies and gentlemen, these important affairs require years of experience in supervising the labor of hundreds of willing hands."

Alexander laughed and said, "Hear! Hear!" and Sallie and Alice clapped noisily.

Then it was Eudocia's turn to mount a chair and present a brief disquisition on the spanking of naughty children. "Spare the rod," she said, looking fiercely down at Horace, "and spoil the child." Horace quailed, but when everyone laughed, he did, too.

Then Sallie bounced up on her chair and delivered a fiery endorsement of the opinions of Mrs. Stanton on the enslavement of womankind by their husbands, fathers, and brothers. "Me, I'm never going to get married," cried Sallie, jumping down.

"Speaking as the only married man at this table," said Alexander, "I am insulted." Then he hoisted his nine-year-old sister-in-law up on her chair. "Your turn, Alice." Alice looked blank and clutched her doll.

"Tell us about Amelia, Alice dear," said Ida.

The laughter from the dining room drifted up through Eben's open window. He was bent over his writing table, composing a letter to a possible future speaker. It was short and, in Eben's opinion, too flowery.

> *My dear sir,*
> *The undersigned writes to request the favor of a Lyceum lecture to be delivered in the Town Hall of Nashoba on the 15th of September on any topic you choose, the sum of $25 to be the honorarium.*
>
> > *Sir, I am your obedient servant,*
> > *Eben Flint,*
> > *Sec'y, Nashoba Lyceum*

Next morning, by a stroke of astonishing good fortune, Horatio Biddle happened to enter the Nashoba post office just as Eben Flint slipped his letter under the bars of the postmaster's window. Stepping forward to take his turn, Horatio could not help seeing the address on the envelope. Glancing over his shoulder, he saw the young man open the door and step outside. Postmaster Phineas Wilder was hitching up his pants and looking the other way. Swiftly, without a twinge of conscience, Horatio reached out to retrieve Eben's letter, because it was addressed to—

> *Dr. Oliver Wendell Holmes, Esq.*
> *164 Charles Street*
> *Boston, Massachusetts.*

A Pretty Fair Steeple

Eben, too, had heard the rumor about Josiah's sacred edifice, but he said nothing as he helped stack the boards behind Josiah's barn. All six and a half thousand board feet of pale, sweet-smelling lumber had been carted into the back corner of Josiah's lot and dumped in clattering heaps among the blackberry canes. Every single piece of milled wood must now be stacked, each layer separated from the next with sticks. The boards looked ready to go, but they were not. In order that they not warp and shrink, they had to dry for a couple of months.

The stacking had to be accomplished in the long twilight of June evenings. During working hours, Eben was busy supervising the construction of a Baptist church in Waltham. And Josiah Gideon was kept on the move in response to crisis after crisis in the almshouses under his jurisdiction. An overseer in the town of Bexley reported the maltreatment of feebleminded women by a matron, and there had been an urgent letter from the superintendent of an asylum in Hudson, where one insane inmate had attacked another with a knife. Therefore, only Julia, Isabelle, and James were at home in the Gideon household during the day. The two women sometimes left the house to do errands here and there, but James was always at home.

One noonday, alone in the house, James stood in the high open doorway at the back of the barn, looked out at the heaps of lumber waiting to be stacked, and stepped out into the sunlight.

Isabelle's errands and Julia's visiting kept them away half the afternoon. When Isabelle came home at last, she went at once to the kitchen to put down her basket. Hearing a clatter from outside, she glanced out the window and was surprised to see a familiar-looking man working among the towers of boards in the backyard. Who was it? Then with a lurch in her breast, she recognized the fine head and strong back of her husband, James. It was James as he had been before going off to war.

With confused longing, Isabelle watched him lift one board after another with his iron hooks and drop them neatly into place on one of the stacks. But the sunny backyard was not screened by a line of trees. Isabelle worried that James might be seen by inquisitive passersby on Quarry Pond Road. When her mother came to stand at the window beside her, Isabelle murmured, "He should come in."

Julia watched for a moment in silence and then said, "Let him be."

Later in the afternoon, when Josiah and Eben walked into the backyard, they found someone else stacking boards, not James, but Dickie Doll. "Thank you kindly, Dickie," said Josiah, throwing off his coat.

Dickie winked at Eben. "Sorry, boys, but I ain't doing this for nothing. You got to pay me. A few leftover bits and pieces of these fine chestnut boards, that's all I want. Say, Reverend Gideon, there was a little birdie whispered something in my ear."

"Never mind little birdies," said Josiah, grinning at him.

"Oh, but there was two little birdies. One birdie told me what you intend to manufacture with this here wood."

Josiah picked up a board and shifted his hands until it balanced. "What did the other birdie say?"

Dickie laughed so hard, he had to wipe his face with his neckerchief. "It was pastor's wife. Miz Biddle says there won't never be another steeple in the town of Nashoba."

Dickie went away chuckling. Josiah smiled at Eben and lifted his board to the top of a stack. Eben picked up a wood chip, tossed it high, caught it in his hat, and said, "Sir, I could draw you a pretty fair steeple."

Their Masterpiece

No good, Jack," said Jake, lifting the curtain and coming out of the darkness with a dripping glass plate. "Balloon, she was whipping along too fast."

The aerial view of Concord's Milldam was a blur. "Too bad, Jake," said Jack.

Jake ducked back into the darkness, dropping the curtain behind him. Five minutes later, he came out with another plate in his hand and a broad smile on his face. "Looky here, Jack," he said, holding it up in the sunlight.

Jack gazed at it with his artist's eye. "Truly beauteous, Jake. What town is that? I forget."

"That there's Nashoba, Jack. See the big tree stump? Remember that there stump?"

"I sure do, Jake. Biggest old stump I ever beheld."

Jake took back the plate and looked at it proudly. "This here's our masterpiece, Jack. We got to spread it around."

"Mayors and selectmen, they got to see it, Jake. City councillors and so on. They take one look, they'll all want aerial views of their own premises, courtesy of Jack and Jacob Spratt."

"What about newspapers, Jack? *Evening Transcript? Boston Advertiser?* Whoopsie, I forgot. This here's a photograph."

"I'll copy it, Jake. An engraving. Newspapers, they'll print an engraving."

Jake laughed and slapped his brother on the back. It was clear that the inborn talents of the Spratt brothers—Jake's mechanical genius and Jack's nimble artistic fingers—were complementing each other once again.

It took Jack a week to turn the darks and lights of Jake's masterful photograph into spidery cross-hatchings. Then it was another week before the masterpiece of the Spratt brothers appeared on the front page of the *Boston Evening Transcript,* under the heading, ASTONISHING AERIAL VIEW.

The roof and steeple of the Nashoba church showed clearly in the engraving and so did the burying ground, with the great white disk of the fallen tree among the tombstones.

The *Transcript* was an evening paper. Not till midafternoon did a newsboy hustle down Charles Street and toss a copy on the doorstep of number 164. The thump was a signal for the master of the house to hurry downstairs from his study, throw open the door, pick up the paper, and learn, to his horror, of the death by willful murder of his favorite chestnut tree. With an exclamation of disgust, Dr. Oliver Wendell Holmes, medical man, poet, raconteur, and worshiper of gigantic trees, stared at the engraved view of the lopped stump in the Nashoba burying ground.

The atrocity called for action. Dr. Holmes ran upstairs, sat down at his desk, moved aside his microscope, sharpened his pen, and dipped it in the inkwell. At once, the furious lines came freely, as if flung down by themselves. Stanza after savage stanza

streamed out of his pen in perfect alternating beats of four and
three.

Within the hour, the deed was done. Smiling at the facility
of his genius, Holmes waited only a moment for the ink to dry.
Then he folded his rhymed revenge upon the slayer of the great
Nashoba chestnut and thrust it into an envelope addressed to
"Josephus Gill, Editor, *Boston Evening Transcript.*" Josephus was
an old friend. He would not cavil at this unasked-for submission
from a celebrated contributor. The clever verses would appear
within the week, doubtless on the very first page.

Far away among the outlying villages to the west, delivery of
the *Transcript* was delayed, since it had to be carried by railroad.
At the depot in Concord, it was tossed out of the mail car into a
waiting wagon. Newsboys snatched up bundles for delivery to
Cutler's store on the Milldam and to individual subscribers on
Main Street and all the way out the North Road. Bundles des-
tined for Carlisle, Acton, and Nashoba went by coach.

Therefore, the Nashoba parsonage did not receive a copy of
the paper that had so scandalized Dr. Holmes until the next
morning. Horatio Biddle unfolded the paper at the breakfast
table and gasped at the masterpiece of the brothers Spratt. There
it was in black and white, their aerial view of the Nashoba
churchyard. The glaring round spot in the center was the stump
of the murdered tree.

NOW

Bedford Steeples

I do not propose to discuss here the movements that led to the separation. . . . Much there was that was painful.

—Bedford memoir, 1879

A Great Tidal Wave

There were two old Protestant churches in the town of Bedford. Mary and Homer visited both. Neither of the churches disgorged any morsels of controversial (or perhaps even scandalous) history, but it was an interesting day on the whole.

In the Congregational church, nobody was on hand but a middle-aged man pushing a trolley of folding chairs. "How do you do?" he said graciously, pulling the trolley to a stop with a thudding of chair against chair. "Name's Baker, church sexton."

"How do you do, Mr. Baker," said Homer. "We're Mary and Homer Kelly. We're looking into the histories of churches around here."

"Well, I'm sorry nobody's around but me," said the sexton.

"Perhaps, Mr. Baker," said Homer, "you're a history buff yourself?"

The sexton shook his head. "Sorry, folks. My spiritual home is the Church of Jesus Christ of Latter-day Saints."

Mary said thank you, and so did Homer, but he was disappointed. How could he write the damned book without more information of a fairly sizzling nature? "Mr. Baker," he said, refusing to give up, "I don't suppose you know whether this church had a connection with the poet Oliver Wendell Holmes?" The sexton looked blank. "Or a big tree of some sort?" Mr. Baker shook his head. "Or a lost church? Did you ever hear a story about a lost church in the town of Bedford?"

"Come to think of it," said Mr. Baker, "I saw one just last week."

"You did!" said Mary.

"Where?" said Homer.

"You shoulda been there. Earth opened up and swallowed it right before my eyes."

Homer's face fell. Mary grinned politely and said, "Oh sure."

"Say, Mr. Kelly," said the sexton, "you're not the writer, are you? Did you write that book about chickens?"

"Well, yes, I did." Homer was pleased as usual, but in his wife's presence, he had to avoid vainglory. "You've read it? My *Hen and Chicks*?"

"Well, no, but I just happen to raise a little poultry myself, Plymouth Rocks mostly. I guess I don't need another how-to book."

"Oh, Mr. Baker," said Mary quickly, "may we help ourselves to some of these nice pamphlets?"

The other Protestant church in Bedford was only a few blocks away. They stood on the lawn, staring up at the tall, bluff facade of Bedford's First Parish, a Unitarian house of worship.

"Handsome," said Homer.

"They're all handsome," said Mary.

This time, they were met by an old gentleman in whiskers who introduced himself as Robert Tucket. "But please, dear people, call me Bob."

"Well, good, Bob. My name's Homer. This is my wife, Mary." Then Homer added ignobly, hoping his name might ring a bell, "Kelly, that is. We're Mary and Homer Kelly."

Ah! It did! Bob looked dazzled. His whiskers trembled with awe as he stuttered, "You're not—"

Mary stuck an elbow in Homer's side, but he couldn't help grinning and saying smugly, "Well, yes, I guess I am."

"My God, I never thought I'd have the honor of meeting you in person."

Homer would have said, Aw, shucks, but it was soon apparent that Bob had an entirely different great man in mind.

"That hundred-yard dash back in '65? End of fourth quarter, Scranton a goal behind, then, glory be!" Bob raised his hands in ecstasy.

There was a bewildered pause, and then Mary said dryly, "I think, Bob, you're talking about Harry Kelly. It was Harry who was the football star, not Homer."

"Oh my God, excuse me."

But after delivering this crushing blow, Bob turned out to be a knowledgeable tour guide. He led them into every corner of the elegantly appointed church and explained its early history in elaborate detail, precisely quoting bits and pieces of significant sermons.

Once again, it was the same old story. The original eighteenth-century parish had split in two when the Unitarian heresy came along to shock the orthodox with its strange notions, while the adherents of Calvinism insisted on the old root-and-branch doctrines of divine predestination, human depravity, limited atonement, visible saints, and irresistible grace—and therefore there were now two church steeples in the town of Bedford.

"Which side kept the original building?" asked Homer, flipping over a page of his notebook.

"We did," said Bob. "Congregationalists, they moved down the street."

"I see," said Homer. "How—um—do the two congregations get along now?" Hopefully, he added, "Any lingering bitterness? Any—um—discord?"

"Of course not. Oh, in the beginning, sure." Bob stroked his whiskers and recited a passage by heart: " 'Much there was that was painful, but it was the result of a great tidal wave of changing opinions sweeping over this whole region.' I mean, that's the way they saw it."

" 'A great tidal wave,' of course," said Mary. "Homer knows all about that kind of thing, don't you, Homer?"

"You see, I wrote a book all about it," said Homer, eager to brag at last.

"No kidding," said Bob. In the vestry, he swept up a heap of pamphlets and thrust them at Homer. "I just happen to have written some of these myself. Take them with my compliments."

The Knitting Ministry

H omer took the wheel on the way back to Concord while
Mary riffled through the papers in her lap. To her surprise,
they turned out to be as revealing of the nature of the two Bedford churches as their ancient histories. She was fascinated.
"You know what, Homer, this is what we've been looking for
all the time. Here they are, these two congregations, naked and
exposed."

"Naked!" Homer glanced quickly at the glossy pamphlets
and the stapled sheaves of green and pink paper. "You don't
mean—"

"Oh, Homer, don't be disgusting. I mean they display the at-
titudes of the two congregations, their points of view, their whole
entire—"

"Overarching philosophical turns of mind?"

"Well, I suppose so. Anyway, they're just so typical and revealing. Here they are, these two congregations of good people, equally the spiritual descendants of the Puritan fathers, both of them publicly displaying their inmost churchly hearts and souls, warts and all. Listen to this, Homer. Guess which one this is."

Mary sifted through the photocopies and read from a pink list. " 'Learning God's good news. Prayer concerns and joys. Please remember these people in your daily prayers. Make music with the Lord. Bible Sunday. Moms' Book Group. The Knitting Ministry.' " Mary paused and held up a picture. "Look at all these happy people with their casseroles and paper napkins and balloons. It's a family church supper. Isn't it nice? Okay, which church is it?"

Homer glanced at the photograph. "They look to me like good, devoted, hardworking Congregationalists. Prayer and God and the Bible and family values front and center, right?"

"Are you sure? All right, here's the other one." Mary plucked out another list. " 'Globalization study. Urban ministry. Interfaith couples. A hearty welcome to lesbians and gays. A just economic community. Multicultural leadership training. Singing as an act of compassion. Wellness Institute. Forum on the arts. Spirituality and justice. Intergenerational potluck and circle dancing.' "

"Well, that's easy." Homer laughed. "Speaking as a compassionate old multicultural circle dancer myself, I'd say they're a bunch of heretical Unitarians."

"Of course they are. But isn't it strange—they're both such a long way from their original beliefs, whether it was the single nature of God or the doctrine of original sin. So tell me, which great spiritual leader is whirling faster in his grave, Jonathan Edwards or Ezra Ripley?"

"There must be a high rpm in both cases." Homer edged the car down the switchbacks of their steep driveway. "And I can't help wondering if we're really any better off with our globalization studies and knitting ministries. I mean, we may be a little nearer to the raw truth, but haven't we lost something at the same time? You know, in majestic old philosophical dignity? Jonathan Edwards was a great man."

"But surely, Homer, it's better to be right, even if ruefully, rather than majestically wrong?"

"Well, maybe so. "Homer turned off the engine and sat gazing for a moment at the blue expanse of Fairhaven Bay. "He liked spiders."

"Spiders? Who liked spiders?"

"Jonathan Edwards. He knew an awful lot about spiders." Sighing, Homer heaved himself out of the car. "His doctrine of original sin may be gone for good, but his spiders are true forever."

1868

"There Shall Be No Other Steeple in the Town of Nashoba!"

What degenerate days are these!

—Marcus Tullius Cicero,
"First Oration Against
Catiline"

No Cathedral

It was clear to Josiah that his rebellious new church would be no cathedral. When every board cut from the chestnut logs in the sawmill of Isaac Pole had been stacked in Josiah's backyard, he took a pencil from behind his ear and calculated the total number of board feet. With Isabelle's hens stepping around his feet, he scribbled figures on one of the clean white boards. "Fair-size chicken house, that's all we'll get," he told Eben sadly.

"There are plenty more small trees in the woods," said Eben. "We can cut as many as we need, only they ought to be felled right away so they'll be dry at the same time.'

Eben's supervision of the church construction in Waltham was finished at last, but now he was charged with erecting a large house for a wealthy citizen of Concord. It was to be an elegant mansion in the Italianate style, complete with veranda and servants hall. Only in his free time could Eben draft plans for Josiah Gideon. Josiah's church was far simpler, but even so, it had a steeple. Eben had sketched an open bell chamber with a pyramidal roof over the front door.

One evening, eager to take a look at Eben's plan, Josiah appeared at his door.

As usual, the house was swarming with miscellaneous activity. Eben's brother-in-law, Dr. Clock, was instructing Eben's younger brother, Josh, in the properties of a right-angled triangle, but he jumped up and went to the door in answer to Josiah's knock. Eben's sister Ida hurried away with her howling baby, his sister Sallie ran out of the kitchen to see who was at the door, and Eben's mother, Eudocia, called down a welcome from upstairs, where she was putting Alice to bed. Only Eben's nephew, Horace, was quiet, because he was sound asleep.

"In here, sir, if you please," said Eben. He led Josiah into the dining room and unrolled his plans on the table. Holding down the corners with two teapots, a pitcher, and a pickle dish, Eben grinned at Josiah and quoted the words of Mrs. Gideon: "There shall be no other steeple in the town of Nashoba."

Josiah spread his hands on the table and leaned over Eben's plans and elevations. His whiskers brushed the paper, his quick eyes looked at every detail, and his mind instantly grasped the whole. "Good," he cried, thumping his fist on the table, bouncing the teapots.

Upstairs, Horace woke up. The shout from downstairs was a call to action. He scrambled to his feet on the bed and began jumping up and down. Bouncing on the bed was forbidden, but he couldn't stop, because the springs were making such a fine *whangety-whang* and the bed was shaking so violently and banging against the wall.

"No, no, Horace," cried his grandmother, running in from the next room.

Whimpering, Horace crawled back under the covers. Eudocia

picked up his storybook, sat down on the edge of his bed, and read him "The Three Billy Goats Gruff":

> The youngest Billy Goat crossed the bridge.
> "Trip, trap! Trip, trap!" went the bridge.
> Beneath the bridge lived a terrible troll.
> It roared at the Billy Goat,
> "I'm coming to gobble you up!"

Horace soon fell asleep, but his fingers were so tightly wound in his grandmother's apron that she had to uncurl them one by one.

"Two months it will take for those boards to dry," said Josiah as Eben rolled up his plans. "But the foundation needs to be dug. We can get busy on the hole right away."

Pillars of the Church

Josiah's woodlot on the Acton Turnpike was only a half mile from his house. He had chosen a clearing not far from the road, a little glade empty of trees. On the following Saturday afternoon, he walked down the road, pushing a wheelbarrow laden with shovels, spades, and a keg of ground limestone as white as new-fallen snow.

Eben arrived a moment later with a cartload of short boards, tools, a bucket of nails, and a couple of sawbucks. At once, he began slapping up a crude toolshed, while Josiah used his foot rule to lay out a rough shape in the grass. When he had sifted through his fingers a trail of white limestone all the way around, he gave an excited shout: "Eben, come and look."

Eben put down his saw and stood beside Josiah to admire the

white rectangle in the weedy grass. It was the ragged outline of a single large room. The white square at the far end was the woodshed. No longer was the new church a heroic fancy. There it lay on the ground. The straggling white line proclaimed the existence of a second parish church in the town of Nashoba. Simultaneously, they looked up, as if they could see the entire building, tall and complete, steeple and all.

"Hark," said Eben, "methinks I hear the bell." But then he picked up a heavy fork and handed it to Josiah. "Four feet down, Josiah. The hole's got to be four feet deep so the frost won't heave the whole thing out of plumb."

"Right you are," said Josiah, and he flung himself at the task. Setting his boot on the fork, he tried to thrust it deep into the earth. But instead of sinking to the top of the tines, it struck a rock. Feverishly Josiah levered up the rock and sank the fork in again. This time, it was caught in a choking tangle of roots.

"I'll go kitty-corner," said Eben, and he carried his fork and spade to the far end. It was clear that every chunk of earth in the clearing would have to be wrenched up and pried out.

They worked at the formidable task all afternoon. Occasionally, a passerby glanced at them curiously. One of them turned off the road to pass the time of day. "What you fellas up to? What you got down there, a treasure chest?"

Eben looked at Josiah and said nothing. Josiah went on digging, but with a dash of bravado he said, "It's a church. We're building a new church."

"A church!" The man was dumbfounded. "But this here's Nashoba, ain't it? You folks already got a church." He looked at them accusingly. "This here ain't gonna be no goddamned popish chapel?' When Josiah glowered, the stranger backed away. "Sorry, gentlemen, didn't mean no offense."

So the news went by zigs and zags from one astonished ear to another, until it reached the parsonage of the Reverend Horatio Biddle. Horatio was struck dumb. Recovering, he jumped up from his chair, clapped on his hat, threw open the front door, crossed the green at a gallop, and raced along the Acton Turn-pike.

By the time he pulled up, gasping, at the clearing in Josiah Gideon's woodlot, six men in shirtsleeves were prying up the dirt, digging down deep, slowly cutting out the corners of a rectangle in the ground. Horatio backed away in dismay. The rumor was true. They were carving out the foundation of a new church, a rival church, an outrageous church that had no right to exist.

To Horatio's mortification, he saw that four of the men digging the foundation were not madmen like Josiah Gideon nor out-of-towners like young Eben Flint. Horatio knew them all by name. They were Artemus Grout, Joseph Hunt, Theodore Wilbur, and Samuel Brooks. They were members of his own congregation. No, not merely members—they were pillars. All four of them were stalwart pillars of Nashoba's First Parish Church.

Jolly Old Dickens

The sweet airs of spring were gone. It was midsummer, hot and close. The rain held off. Kitchen gardens and orchards suffered, but the corn grew apace. It was fine weather for haying and for drying fresh-cut wood.

"Another week," said Josiah, tapping one of the planks piled up behind his house. "By the time I'm back from touring all the almshouses in the southern part of the county, these boards will be fit and ready to go."

The clearing in Josiah's woodlot was no longer a clearing. Cartloads of topsoil had been carried away to improve an impoverished acre here and there, but heaps of sandy subsoil still remained beside the cellar hole. All the rocks had been hurled to one side after they were pulled out of the ground, then picked up again to line the foundation. Leftover stones cluttered the edge of the woods, along with a boulder dragged out of the hole by the team of oxen belonging to Joseph Hunt.

Behind the boulder stood the toolshed, finished by Eben in a couple of evenings. "I could have slapped it up quicker," he told Josiah, "if I hadn't been slapping mosquitoes at the same time."

The window glass had come. Eben's order had been filled far too early, and the three heavy crates lay unopened behind the toolshed. Part of Josiah's pretty woodlot was now a wasteland of stumps, the wreckage of trees felled to eke out the supply of lumber. A straw bonnet hung forgotten in a brush pile, a lost doll leaned against a stump, and a rubber ball that had streaked away from Eben's nephew, Horace, lay among last year's fallen leaves.

When Josiah came back from inspecting the shoddy appointments of the almshouses at the extreme southern border of Middlesex County, he declared with an exultant shout that the stacked wood was dry. At last, the construction of his defiant little church could begin in earnest.

Not much could be expected in the month of August from the farmers among Josiah's supporters. But other men had time to spare. Alexander Clock's patients were always healthier in summer than in winter, and he often accompanied Eben to lend a hand. All the district schoolhouses in Nashoba and Concord were locked up and empty, except for a few droning flies. Pupils and schoolmasters were free to help out. Even Professor Eaton no longer traveled by rail to Cambridge to give instruction in the *Eclogues* of Virgil, and the court cases in which lawyer Jarvis Brown was concerned had been reduced to one (about which he did not speak).

But the construction of even so small a building called for many hours of Eben's time. As its designer, he had to furnish measurements for sills, corner posts, cross beams, and rafters. And no one else but Eben could direct the layout of the timbers on the ground and mark precisely for the amateur carpenters the places to cut the mortises and tenons that were to hold the framework together.

Sometimes Eben was so beset that he wanted to harden his heart and take off for some other corner of the world. But soon his resolve would be restored by the ardent look on Josiah's face as he hewed a beam with a broad ax or pressed his knee on a board to send his excited saw wheezing back and forth.

And there was also a strange exhilaration in visiting Josiah's house whenever new boards had to be carted to the woodlot from the stacks in his backyard.

They were comfortable together now—Eben and Isabelle, Eben and James. One day in early August, Eben found Isabelle reading aloud to James a novel by Charles Dickens. "Oh, good," said Eben, "jolly old Charles Dickens," and he sat down to listen to the story with James.

But the passage she had been reading was not very jolly. "It's such a sad story," said Isabelle, apologizing to Eben. "Perhaps you'd rather not hear the last page."

"What, *A Tale of Two Cities?*" said Eben. "But it's a very fine book."

So Isabelle looked down and went on reading to James the sublime last thought of Sydney Carton as he stood on the scaffold. *"It is a far, far better thing that I do, than I have ever done; it is a far, far better rest that I go to than I have ever known."*

Swashbuckling Insurrection

On any sunny day in August, ten or fifteen defectors from Horatio Biddle's congregation would be present in the clearing to help with the raising of Josiah's church. Only a few were skilled at rough carpentry, but all of them followed directions and worked together in a giddy spirit of high-principled and swashbuckling insurrection. It was men's work, but the women arrived at lunchtime with lunch pails and picnic baskets. Every midday was like a festive Sunday nooning.

Julia Gideon came every other day, taking turns with Isabelle. Julia's basket was always full of good things, but she had no heart for the high spirits and laughter of the others. Everything Julia feared seemed about to happen. She had heard a terrible rumor: Ingeborg Biddle had gone to law.

But look at Josiah! Just look at him! The wolves were gathering, and yet he was flinging himself into the work, rejoicing in the lifting of every timber, careless of who might legally own that particular measured board, whether church, town, commonwealth, or God on high. Every morning, he bounded out of bed at cockcrow, kissed her, and went rollicking off down the Acton Turnpike with a slab of bread in his hand.

Oh, yes, it was a great work; Julia knew that. The whole undertaking was a kind of metaphorical revolution: The murdered tree would live again as a house of God. Her husband's obsession was dangerous, his excitement too wild and uncontrolled, and yet Julia was helpless to interfere. She could do nothing but play a woman's part.

It was high summer in Nashoba. Every day, Julia stripped the kitchen garden. The pole beans were coming on thick and fast, and so were the beets, the cucumbers for pickling, the summer squash, the watermelons. The potatoes were invisible underground but Julia knew they were there, and later on she would fork them up in clusters, the Early Rose, the Green Mountain. The squash vines were yielding a bumper crop, and tiny ears were showing on the cornstalks. The blueberries had gone by in the shady woods, but the blackberries were ripe. Isabelle and Julia waded into sunny thickets and came home with scratched hands and brimming pails.

And every day in the sweltering heat of August, Julia fired up the stove for the baking of velvet cakes and gingerbread. She brewed tea in jars, wrapped them in newspapers, and cooled them in the cellar before packing them into the basket.

For Isabelle, these journeys were excursions, respites from her care of James. But whenever she took the loaded basket from her mother, the two women exchanged a sober glance. Isabelle's meant, Be good to him; Julia's, Of course I will.

Returning home, Isabelle brought stories to James about the events of the day. "Mr. Pease tipped over on the ladder this morning. He wasn't hurt, but he said things we ladies weren't supposed to hear." James made a chuckling noise in his throat. "Ella Viles caught her skirt on a nail and it fell right off. There she stood in her petticoat! How she blushed! James, do you remember Ella Viles?" James shook his head. But when Isabelle described Ella's curls and ribbon bows, he nodded, remembering.

But sometimes Isabelle's encounters with Ella Viles were not to be described at home. One day, Ella unpacked her basket and, casting a significant glance at Isabelle, said, "It's for Eben."

"Oh?" Isabelle still found it hard to believe that Eben could be so foolish. "Did he like your photograph?"

Ella giggled. "Oh yes." Leaning closer to Isabelle, she whispered, "He keeps it next to his heart."

"He does?" Then Isabelle couldn't help asking, "How do you know?"

Ella rolled her eyes and simpered, "Oh, I know."

Horrid visions appeared to Isabelle, and she said no more.

On the third Saturday in August, the sun shone as always through the remaining trees in the woodlot, dappling the clearing with round spots of light. And once again at noon, the rugs and tablecloths were spread out all over the rough grass. Abby Whittey leaned against a stump, shelling hard-boiled eggs. On a checkered shawl, Eloise Stearns opened a napkin and handed warm rolls to the little girls curled up beside her, their skirts flounced out like china dolls.

Eben's sister Ida had come from Concord to watch her husband as he worked in his shirtsleeves with the others. She was amused to see the awkwardness of Alexander's clever doctoring hands. The saws of the other men whizzed swiftly through board or beam, while Alexander's bucked and stuck fast.

Smiling, Ida laid Gussie down on the blanket in the shade while Horace romped with the other little boys, screaming joyfully in the discovery that there were other beings in the world like himself.

Professor Eaton came nearly every day to inspire the builders

with architectural examples from classical times. He brought
no food for himself, but he was always well supplied with delica-
cies from the women's baskets. Yesterday, brushing cake crumbs
from his coat, he had taken Eben aside in order to describe in
detail the Tuscan villa of Pliny the Younger. Later, he enlight-
ened Samuel Brooks on the history of Grecian temple construction while Mr. Brooks cut to size the last long boards for
the floor. And throughout the long afternoon as David Kibbee sat
patiently riving shingles with a drawknife, he was lectured on the
tepidarium, calidarium, and *frigidarium* of the Baths of Caracalla.

Today the food was laid out and ready on the blankets, but
the work did not stop. With a count of "One, two, three," ten
men hoisted the entire framework of the south side halfway up,
supported on their humped backs, and then at the shout of
"Now," they heaved it upright and braced it to the sill. Then,
hooting and laughing, they walked across Sam's new-laid floor,
wiping their hands on their pants. Josiah folded up his long legs
and sat down beside Isabelle.

Only Eben Flint did not join the others. He stayed high on a
ladder, augering a hole for a mortised joint.

Isabelle watched his intent face and deft hands. Ella Viles
watched, too, but she was tired of waiting. Jumping up from her
pretty display of cold tongue and sponge cake, she called out
sweetly, "Eben, dear, come down."

The other women stared at her in surprise, but Eben did not
look her way. Instead, he darted a quick glance at Isabelle. His
face was hot and red as he lifted a heavy beetle to drive the
treenail home and pin the joint together.

The nooning was over. The ladies scrubbed the sticky faces
of their children, gathered up their pickle jars and eggshells and
leftover cakes, shook out their blankets, and set off for home.

Ella's good things had not been tasted, but she giggled as she
repacked her basket. Then she took Isabelle's arm as if they
were the greatest of chums and whispered secrets in her ear all
the way home.

Behind them in the clearing, the men went back to work. Axes were honed, window frames roughed out, holes drilled with brace and bit. Eben was pleased to discover that George Blood knew how to clamp a narrow board in a curve. "You can't have a house of worship without you got pointy windows," said George. "Ain't that right, Eben?"

Eben laughed and said it was right; in fact he had drawn pointed windows on his plan. "See there?" Then Eben and Josiah were surprised when another carpenter appeared just as the other men gathered up their tools and set off down the Acton Turnpike.

It was old Dickie Doll from the Nashoba Home Farm. "The pulpit, Reverend Gideon," said Dickie, taking Josiah by the front of his shirt. "I'll make you the grandest pulpit ever was seen."

Is Humanity Depraved?

Ingeborg Biddle was a woman of spirit, fearless in her pursuit of the truth. Surely in this case it would prevail, she told herself. But so far, the pursuit had been stalled—her investigation of the history of the burying ground and the actual ownership of the precious wood from the fallen tree. To whom did it actually belong? The parish records went back only as far as the year 1828, when a fire had destroyed the first edifice. That avenue was closed. And her research into the rights of the town in this case was hindered because the town clerk was a fool.

"We got nothing here, ma'am," he told Ingeborg. "Guess you'll have to consult the Registry of Deeds."

"And where, pray, is the Registry of Deeds?"

The town clerk gestured vaguely at the window. "It's in

Cambridge, ma'am, way to the east in Cambridge. Never been that far myself. Boston coach don't go that way. Of course, ma'am, you could take the train at the Concord depot, but the cars don't go that way, neither. You have to change someplace or other." He threw up his hands. "I fear I am not acquainted with Cambridge transport."

Scornfully, Ingeborg retorted, "You make it sound as impossible as finding the Northwest Passage."

"Where's that, ma'am? Never been there myself."

Ingeborg stalked out of the town hall. Surely the human mind had devised a way of crossing the barren wastes of the city of Cambridge from one side to the other. But for now, the journey must wait. There was too much to do at home.

For one thing, there was the next meeting of her *conversazione*. What subject should the ladies be told to discuss? Ingeborg sat at her desk, sucking the feathery tip of her pen, and at once a topic occurred to her. Swiftly, she scribbled it down: "Is humanity depraved, or is there a potential for goodness in every human breast?"

It didn't take long to make up her own mind about human depravity. The next church service settled the matter.

The weather continued fine, which was lucky for the work on Josiah Gideon's rambunctious new church, but unlucky for everything else. Wells threatened to go dry. Crops lay parched in the field. But Josiah's little building grew taller in the sunshine every day, like the growing tree it had once been. On the last Sunday morning in August, a small bell was swayed up in the new steeple, complete with bell rope and wheel.

Eben had found it among the effects of a dismantled church in Watertown and bought it, he said, for a song. Now he knelt in the open bell chamber and fed the end of the rope through the opening in the ceiling. Josiah reached up from below and pulled it down.

The bell jangled, competing with another loud reverberation

from farther up the road. The bell in the steeple of the First Parish was ringing to summon the congregation. That bell was bigger than this one, and its peal was louder and more musical, sounding far over the town and the surrounding fields, bonging dimly even in the robing room of the Reverend Horatio Biddle.

But as Horatio adjusted the folds of his ministerial gown, he stiffened at the sound of an unfamiliar clanging from the direction of the Acton Turnpike, a rude noise that interfered with the noble chiming of the bell in his own steeple. At once he guessed that Josiah Gideon was ringing a mutinous bell in the crude little shack he called a church. Listening to the crisscrossing clash of the two bells, Horatio told himself that he had nothing to fear. The God-fearing citizens of Nashoba would surely know which bell was calling them to blessedness and which to godlessness and anarchy. Timidly, he peered at his congregation through a peephole in the door.

Something was terribly wrong. Where were they? Horatio could see only a scattering of elderly women and the sad relics who walked to church every Sunday from the Home Farm. His wife was there, of course, sitting firmly upright in the Biddle family pew. She was staring straight ahead, contemplating the nature of human depravity.

Well, at least his old friend Professor Jedediah Eaton was walking into his pew, just as usual. Like Horatio, Jedediah was an ardent Latin scholar. The two of them enjoyed exchanging jocular Latin tags—Caesar's famous exclamation when he saw his friend Brutus among the assassins, *Et tu, Brute?* or some cutting remark by Cicero. Oh, yes, thank God for Jedediah, but where was everyone else?

Horatio pulled out his watch and held it to his ear. Had it stopped? No, but surely it was running too fast. Perhaps the actual time was only half-past ten? Usually by quarter to eleven, he could hear the shuffle of feet, the subdued murmur of voices, and the creaking of pews as his parishioners sat down. In the winter, there was also the cheerful noise of wood being chucked

into the stoves and the pinging of the stovepipe as it expanded
with hot air, but this morning the stoves were cold and the
stovepipe silent.

In fact, there was no noise at all from the sanctuary. Horatio
jumped back as the door opened and his wife slipped in, her
tight smile vanishing as she closed the door behind her.

Ingeborg's face was white, her hands were shaking, and her
whisper was hoarse and desperate. "It's that wicked traitor Gideon.
He's kidnapped the congregation."

The Doom of Leadership

The Reverend Horatio Biddle sat alone in his study, the door closed against his wife and the servant girl. Once again, he was looking for a certain half-remembered passage, but in what book had he seen it? His desk was heaped with weighty volumes.

Turning the pages of one after another, he found it at last in Charles Cuthbert Hall's great spiritual outpouring, *Ministerial Power*:

> He who has borne the burden and heat of the day learns in bitterness of soul the doom of leadership. To stand in the midst of the ecclesia, with the ordinary vicissitudes of man's life transpiring upon one's self from day to day, its variations of mental activity, its episodes of spiritual depression, its yoke

of earthly care, its fettering relationships, and yet to behold a
thousand souls assembled and waiting for inspiration . . . that
is the doom of leadership.

Oh, yes, that was Horatio Biddle's present case—"bitterness
of soul, the doom of leadership." Horatio put his palms down
flat on the open book and lowered his forehead until it rested on
his hands, for his condition was even worse.

If only there had been in his own congregation that morning
"a thousand souls assembled and waiting for inspiration." Alas,
the only souls waiting for inspiration from Horatio Biddle had
been the flotsam from the Home Farm, the Widow Poole, the
Misses Rochester, deaf old Dora Mills, the sexton, and, of
course, dear Jedediah Eaton. Horatio's wife, Ingeborg, didn't
count. Even the choirmistress had played hooky, along with
every one of her screeching sopranos, tenors, altos, and basses.

How dared they abandon him? As their pastor, did he not
have a lofty claim on all those people? Were not their souls his
to entreat, to teach, to ennoble? And did not they, in their turn,
have a loving stake in the church of their fathers, and in the
pews of which they were proprietors? Even in the stabling of
their horses?

That thieving scoundrel Josiah Gideon had alienated the af-
fections of Horatio's favorite parishioners, the leading men and
women of the congregation. Could it possibly be true that he
had captured Frank and Martha Wheeler? George Blood and his
wife, Pearl? Stalwart Samuel Brooks? Sweet Abigail Whittey?
And what about Horatio's old friend District Court Judge
Bigelow and his entire family? "Oh, no, dear God," prayed Horatio, "let it not be true that Sam Bigelow has followed the
beckoning finger of Josiah Gideon."

Then Horatio grasped at a straw. What if Josiah had no legal
right to ensnare a congregation? He called himself "the Reverend," but what if he had never been ordained?

Once again, Horatio riffled the pages of his books until he

found an excellent passage in a splendid work by Dr. Ross: "The local churches are the only organs of the Spirit provided for this work of ordination. They have consequently the highest reasons for keeping out of the ministry all whom the Lord has not qualified and called."

Keeping that fiend in human flesh, Josiah Gideon, out of the ministry, that was what it meant. Horatio stood up eagerly and snatched off the shelf *The Handbook of the Congregational Ministry in Massachusetts*. It was a useful compendium. Horatio often ran his finger down the lists of pastors to find the names of colleagues here and there. Now his finger raced down a page and stopped abruptly at Josiah Gideon's name. Josiah had been ordained in the year 1840 in the First Parish Church of Hemingford, Connecticut. The man was actually a clergyman. He did indeed have the right to an ecclesiastical title.

Disappointed, Horatio threw the book on the floor. He couldn't bear it. He rose from his chair and paced around the room. In his despair, he would have torn his garments, had they not been woven of stout Boston broadcloth. Instead, he laid his suffering head against the plaster forehead of Marcus Tullius Cicero and wept.

> *How much further, Catiline, will you carry your abuse*
> *of our forbearance? What bounds will you set*
> *to this display of your uncontrolled audacity?*
> *Alas! What degenerate days are these!*

> **—Marcus Tullius Cicero, "First**
> **Oration Against Catiline"**

Another Bitter Pill

E ven worse than the humiliating church service on Sunday was Ingeborg's *conversazione* the following Thursday.

Wilhelmina Wilder sent a note by her kitchen maid. "Dearest Ingeborg, I am so sorry, but I am indisposed this afternoon, having taken to my bed."

A creamy envelope from Eugenia Hunt was delivered by her husband's hired man. He arrived at the parsonage door just as Abigail Whittey came up the steps of the front porch. Ingeborg took the envelope, Abigail opened her mouth to say something, then closed it again, and Ingeborg's maid, Millie, scurried past with the cake stand.

"My dear Ingeborg," said Eugenia's note, "I am *désolée* that I cannot attend this afternoon, being afflicted with one of my frightful migraines. I shall spend the afternoon in bed in *stygian darkness,* having drawn the shades."

"Well, it's too bad," said Ingeborg to Abigail, rallying her forces, "it appears that our circle will be a little diminished this afternoon. Minnie and Eugenia have both been taken ill."

"Eugenia?" said Abigail in surprise. "But I saw Eugenia's buggy careering down Quarry Pond Road only a moment ago." Abigail realized at once that she should not have said this, but she went on bravely to deliver her own regrets. "I'm dreadfully sorry, Ingeborg, but I've only stopped by to tell you that a very important engagement has come up, which will prevent my attendance this afternoon."

Abigail had rehearsed this speech, mumbling it over and over on the way to the parsonage, but it did not have the hoped-for effect. Ingeborg's company face changed. She glowered at Abigail, who then whipped out something from under her shawl, thrust it at Ingeborg, and fled, explaining as she scuttled out the door, "I just wondered if you'd seen this."

"Seen what?" Ingeborg stared at the *Boston Evening Transcript.* But at once, two more of her ladies fluttered in and had to be welcomed. With her heart clenched in foreboding, Ingeborg laid the *Transcript* on the hall table and led them into the sitting room, where the topic of the afternoon had been changed from the question about depraved humanity—it was depraved; it most certainly was—to a safer subject: "Poetry sublime."

A circle of three was too small to be called a *conversazione,* especially since Eugenia and Abigail, the cleverest of Ingeborg's friends, were missing. Even frivolous young Ella Viles had not come, although she had failed to send an excuse.

"Cynthia," said Ingeborg, pulling herself together, "I hope you will favor us with your opinion?"

Cynthia Smith jerked upright in her chair and tried to remember the first line of "Ode on a Grecian Urn." She had committed the entire poem to memory, but now under the gelid eye of Ingeborg Biddle, she could remember only one line. "O Attic shape!" gibbered Cynthia, then faltered to a stop. "I'll just read it from the book," she whispered timidly.

Pity Ingeborg Biddle! She was not a stupid woman, and her efforts to raise the intellectual aspirations of the women of Nashoba were surely worthy of praise. Heroically, she explained to silly Cynthia Smith and foolish Dora Mills that the discussion this afternoon was supposed to be concerned with the meaning and value of the poetic instinct, not merely a recitation of favorite verses.

Eugenia and Abigail would have been up to it, but not Cynthia and Dora. They were struck dumb. In desperation, Cynthia reared up from her chair, seized the cake stand, and rushed it across the room to Dora, who stopped up her mouth with macaroons, and then to Ingeborg, who waved it away.

The afternoon was a failure. Not until her guests had made their farewells could Ingeborg plump herself down on the sofa with the newspaper and a piece of cake.

Only then did she understand the pitiful excuses of Minnie, Eugenia, and Abigail. The subject of the afternoon's discussion had been poetry, and this, too, was a poem, but it was a bitter blow.

On the first page of the *Transcript,* the lofty view of Nashoba's burial ground appeared once again, with the white scar of the chestnut stump showing clearly among the tombstones. But this time, there was also a poem by Dr. Oliver Wendell Holmes. It was a parody of Longfellow's "The Village Blacksmith," but at the same time it was a villainous attack on a nameless person who could be none other than the Reverend Horatio Biddle.

> *Under the spreading chestnut tree*
> *A vicious killer stands;*
> *He looks up at the branches free,*
> *A great ax in his hands.*
>
> *The tree flings wide its glorious crown,*
> *Its leaves the winds caress.*

Two hundred years the burial ground
By this tree has been blessed.

But now the madman lifts his ax
To play the devil's part.
The keen blade strikes and strikes again
To burst that mighty heart.

Great nature weeps, Nashoba's jewel
Lies shattered on the ground,
Broken, the hearts of young and old
In all the country round.

Let good men curse the vandal vile
Who killed our ancient tree.
May this foul deed afflict his soul
Till he shall cease to be.

Ingeborg couldn't believe her eyes. Anguished, she read the
dreadful poem again. The "vandal vile" had been her own distinguished husband. Everyone in Nashoba knew it, and soon
everyone in the great cities of Cambridge and Boston would
know it, too. The name of the Reverend Horatio Biddle would
be a byword and a hissing throughout the land—or at least
throughout the Massachusetts counties of Suffolk and Middlesex, which were all of the land that mattered.

Of course it was the fault of Josiah Gideon. And yet—how
strange!—Ingeborg felt a curious hunger rising in her heart.
She longed to run down the hill and across the road, knock on
the Gideons' door, and fling herself into the open arms of Mrs.
Julia Gideon.

Had Horatio seen today's *Transcript*? How wretched it would
make him! The poor man was spending most of his time sequestered in his study.

Horatio was there today, hiding away from Ingeborg and her

ladies, from the tea party and the high tone of the conversation. Once again, he sat at his desk reading Cicero, his spectacles hooked over his ears. Here he could recover from the perfidy of the outside world and be almost happy. As always, Marcus Tullius Cicero could be depended upon to open wide his marble arms and take Horatio to his breast.

The Purloined Parish

Week after week the kidnapping went on, during which time the roof of Josiah's church was shingled, the glass fitted in the window openings, and many other crucial details completed under the direction of Eben Flint.

One dismal Sunday morning, Ingeborg hurried in desperation from the parsonage to the Home Farm and roused out every one of the elderly residents, the slackers as well as the faithful. Old Dickie Doll was not among them, but a dozen others shambled after Ingeborg across the green and into the church.

To them and to another handful of worshipers—Ingeborg's maid, Millie, her cook, the church sexton, and the keeper of the grounds—Horatio Biddle preached. These days, he no longer had the heart to compose new thoughts and order them into a homily that began with Scripture, went on to state a thesis that rose to a rousing climax, and fell away softly to a gentle restatement and a final scriptural passage. This morning, his wife, Ingeborg, winced as she recognized the opening words of Horatio's discourse on the virtues of temperance.

Half a mile away in the clearing beside the Acton Turnpike, the absconding congregation walked into their new house of worship to celebrate its completion. The structure that had been only a visionary shape in the air last June was now sheathed and sealed from the weather. A ladder in one corner led to the bell chamber. The entrance door had been hung in place, and now it carried a wooden shield carved with a tree, the work of Dickie Doll. The interior was still unplastered and the pews were only rough boards, but there were splendid finishing touches. Eudocia Flint had contributed her reed organ, the choirmistress of Horatio Biddle's church had made off with a set of hymnbooks, and David Kibbee had fitted up an iron stove and had hung from the rafters a stovepipe that wrapped itself around three sides of the chamber.

But it was the pulpit that was everyone's pride. Dickie Doll had made it from leftover ends and pieces of chestnut boards. He had cut them to size, clamped them in the jaws of his vise, mitered the edges, and polished the surfaces until they were silk under his hand. Then with buckets of hoof parings from the local smithy, he had boiled up a foul-smelling pot of glue to seal the separate elements into one substance, never to come asunder. Then Dickie's pleasure had begun in earnest. His decorative carving for the pulpit was his masterpiece. The swags of flowers and fruit, the bearded prophets supporting the pediment, and the channeled colonettes at the corners would have done credit to Grinling Gibbons, if Dickie had ever heard of Grinling Gibbons, but of course he had not. The clever fingers chiseling the fine-grained wood had followed pictures in Dickie's own head.

The men and women of the purloined congregation smiled as they sat down on the benches facing this wonder of art. All were in their Sunday best—the men in black coats, the women in bonnets and shawls. In spite of the fine clothes, there was an atmosphere of cutting school, of throwing off a burdensome yoke. In place of churchgoing gravity in a pious hush, there were joyful greetings, shakings of hands, clappings on backs. The small rough building might have been a towering church with a steeple as high as the sky.

This first Sunday in October was as warm as a day in August. Pine knots in a basket were ready to hand, but today there was no need for David Kibbee to set a fire going in the stove. The cheerful members of the new congregation settled themselves on the benches in the fragrance of newly sawn boards. They picked up their hymnbooks, adjusted their coattails, smoothed their skirts, and hushed their children. Professor Eaton had no children, but there were smiles of approval as he sat down. His gray whiskers were an ornament and his distinguished presence flattered the congregation.

Ida and Alexander Clock belonged to the First Parish in Concord, and so did Ida's mother, Eudocia, but they had come with Eben to celebrate the first gathering of the new parish. Young Horace was there, too, wedged between his mother and stepfather. Horace was overawed. He sat in rigid stillness until Mr. Kibbee took hold of the bell rope and pulled it down with all his strength. Then Horace squirmed around to watch Mr. Kibbee's arms rise and fall to make the bell ring harsh and loud.

It rang and rang. Mr. Kibbee was tireless. In the meantime, the rest of the congregation faced forward, looking at the pulpit. In its magnificence, it was like a seal of approval or a document declaring the right of this church to exist.

The bell stopped ringing. Josiah Gideon stood up from the bench where he had been sitting with his wife, stepped forward to the pulpit, and called for prayer.

If the Spratt brothers had been floating over the new building in their balloon, reaching out from the basket to catch
prayers drifting up through the newly shingled roof, they would
have netted dozens that called for a blessing on the new congregation. The only personal supplication was the fervent appeal of
Julia Gideon.

Of course Julia was grateful that her husband's volcanic decision to form a new parish had won the support of so many
friends and neighbors. But what about the lawsuit? Josiah had
seemed entirely unconcerned when the dreaded letter arrived in
the mail. He had tossed it across the table, laughed aloud, and
cried, "See what the fool is up to now."

The letter was a summons to the county court. Josiah was
accused of defiling a graveyard. Julia trembled, and her prayer
turned into a succession of misgivings. How on earth could he
defend himself? It was God's truth that he had dug up and removed the casket of Deacon Sweetser and buried it somewhere
else. How could there be any defense against the truth? And
surely it was only the beginning. Before long, they would accuse
him of the theft of church property, the removal of all the valuable wood from the fallen chestnut tree. And what about the
theft of an entire congregation? The abduction of living men
and women? Julia prayed that Josiah's boisterous excitement
would settle down into the quiet common sense of a man
whose wits were not astray.

The prayer of Julia's daughter, Isabelle, was disjointed. She
found it impossible to concentrate. She had to keep her eyes
tightly shut against the sight of Ella Viles on the bench in front
of her, crowded close to the side of Eben Flint. When Isabelle's
father said "Amen," she opened her eyes and saw Ella looking
back at her with a sly smile.

The time had come for Josiah's sermon. Julia stiffened as her
husband began to speak. But to her relief, he did not gloat in
triumph or indulge in tempestuous exultation. His eyes were
incandescent, but he spoke with the reasoning eloquence of a

seasoned preacher. The burden of his homily was simple. The wooden church they had built with their own hands was a temple whose corner posts were the ethical commandments of Jesus Christ and the Sermon on the Mount. The floor was holy reason, the roof the love of God.

In the hush that followed, Josiah picked up a hymnbook, riffled the pages, and called for "Old Hundred." At once, Eudocia Flint sprang forward. Sitting firmly upright at the organ, she pumped air into the bellows with her feet, thrust out her knees to swell the melodious noise, and ran her fingers up and down the keyboard. Everyone rose to sing.

Josiah closed the service with the psalm about the blessed man whose delight is in the law of the Lord, who is like a tree planted by the rivers of water, a tree that bringeth forth fruit in his season, whose leaf shall not wither.

He said nothing more. He did not have to explain the pretty allegory about the resurrection of the slaughtered tree. The tools of the men had hammered it into the posts and beams, and the mixing spoons of the women had beaten it into their gingerbread. It was common knowledge.

"Et tu, Jedediah?"

When Ingeborg Biddle at last screwed up the courage to show her husband the abominable piece of doggerel in the *Evening Transcript,* Horatio's mortification was complete. He paced the floor, wrung his hands, ground his teeth, and then, suddenly, he bolted.

Ingeborg cried, "Horatio, where are you going?"

He could not speak. Throwing up his arms in anguish, Horatio charged out of the house by the back door. In the kitchen garden, Agnes, the cook, was heaving at an enormous winter squash while her gentleman friend plucked at a banjo. When the master of the house came lurching through the cabbages, Agnes looked up in surprise and the banjo twanged a false note. Horatio stumbled past them, heading for the barn. Before him the great door yawned wide, and within the fragrant darkness one of the carriage horses looked out from its stall at Horatio and stamped and tossed its head.

High above the barn roof rose the familiar domed steeple of Horatio's church. By all the laws of God, that steeple was the property of its pastor. The church belonged to Horatio as surely as the coat on his back, as surely as the burial ground and the accursed chestnut tree, as surely as the souls of his congregation. All of those men and women, by sacred tradition and absolute right, belonged under the fatherly care of the Reverend Horatio Biddle, and under his care alone.

"There shall be no other steeple in the town of Nashoba." Horatio had uttered this decree with solemn authority and his wife had echoed it. And yet now there was indeed another steeple in Nashoba, an absurd joke of a steeple on the ridiculous little shanty that Josiah Gideon called a church, that blaspheming hovel standing so defiantly on a scrubby patch of grass in Josiah's woodlot, right there beside the road to Acton.

During the months when the shanty had been little more than a hole in the ground, Horatio had stayed away, not wanting to show interest in its progress. But sometimes he had crept out at night to fumble through the trees and take a look, hoping to find the whole thing given up as a bad job.

But it had not been given up, and now it was a solid finished building topped by a gimcrack turret with a tinny bell.

And this morning, Horatio had witnessed with his own eyes the defectors from his flock marching straight past the open door of his church to obey the call of that evil little bell. To his dismay, he had seen Douglas Pease stroll by, whistling. Then young Ted Wilbur had sauntered down the road, smoking a cigar. Bitterly, Horatio had watched the familiar runabout of Joseph and Eugenia Hunt wheel blithely down the road, and then the pony trap of the two Miss Rochesters, and finally the splendid equipage of Samuel and Lydia Bigelow.

These apostates were bad enough, but Horatio's heart broke

within his breast when he saw the old-fashioned phaeton of the most distinguished member of his congregation rollicking down the road in the direction of that godless meetinghouse. Even Professor Jedediah Eaton, Horatio's dearest friend and colleague, had been lured away by Josiah Gideon. Horatio felt like Caesar when Brutus appeared among the assassins: *Et tu, Jedediah?*

At the window, Ingeborg watched her despairing husband dart into the barn. Was he about to ride away, to abandon his predicament and leave her forever? And then Ingeborg had a perfidious thought: But would that be so terrible, after all?

No, now he was coming out again, lugging a bale of hay. Ingeborg watched in astonishment as Horatio began tearing it apart and throwing down bundle after bundle. Had he lost his senses? Craning her neck, she saw him shamble away with a single armful, trailing wisps on the ground.

NOW

The Acton Steeple

What is the meaning of life?
(No exceptions, please)

Doaksie Bisbee

You're way down," said Luther Stokes, keeping Homer informed of the bad news every day. "You're second from the bottom. If you don't hurry up with that new whizbang of yours, you'll be gone and forgotten. Have you seen what's on the top of the nonfiction bestseller list right now? A new stunner by Doaksie Bisbee, *You and Your Vagina.*"

"Oh, God," said Homer. "I don't want to hear about my vagina."

"Well, naturally, because you haven't got one. This is strictly for females. I'll bet Mary would be interested. And say, that Doaksie's a cute kid. Have you seen her on TV?"

"Unfortunately, I have actually met the woman."

"No kidding? Well, I suppose all you bestselling writers go to the same snazzy parties."

"Umph," growled Homer. It had not been a party; it had been a shared platform, a horrible experience. He had prepared his speech with care, a dazzling account of the squabbles among Protestant churches in the nineteenth century. He had timed his presentation to the required fifteen minutes, cutting out many a choice paragraph.

Then it was Doaksie's turn. Doaksie had not prepared a speech at all. She had sat on the edge of the platform and talked about her free and easy life—or rather, about the life of her vagina. "Remember the old days," said Doaksie, "when you had to get married to have sex?"

There were screams of laughter, encouraging Doaksie to further intimate revelations. Profoundly pained, Homer sat on his folding chair on the platform and examined the audience closely for the first time. They were mostly young women, very young women. In fact, they reminded him of the rosy-cheeked little girls who were his graduate students.

"Any questions?" asked the moderator, leaping to her feet when Doaksie had exceeded her allotted time by half an hour.

There were dozens of eager questions about sexuality, creativity, and spirituality. At one point, Homer, like a fool, jumped up to complain that words like *creativity and spirituality* were too important to be bandied about. "It should be against the law," he scolded, "to use them more than once a year, or else the word police will get you." There was a feeble titter as he sat down.

Afterward, Homer told Mary that the poet Dante had neglected one of the chief torments of hell. "Pity the unhappy speaker who has to sit in dignified silence while all the questions are addressed to somebody else. Oh, if only I had a vagina to call my own." Groaning piteously, Homer strode across the room to his desk, snatched up a sheaf of papers, and tossed them at the ceiling. "Worthless," he cried. "Not a vagina in the lot."

Mary snatched some of them out of the air, then ran around retrieving the rest from the rubber plant, the lamp shade, and the basket of overdue library books. Two had slithered behind the desk into a snake pit of wires and cables. "Come on, Homer," said Mary, 'we've got to pull this thing away from the wall."

"Way bother?" asked Homer, but he heaved on one end of the desk, and soon all the flying papers were shuffled together in a stack.

Then Mary took Homer by the hand and said, "My poor darling, it's a shame that you don't have a vagina. Tell you what. I've got one." She looked at her watch. "We don't have to leave for that church in Acton for half an hour."

A Semantic Problem

From the road, the church seemed modest enough, a pleasant Victorian building with a small bell tower. But when the car turned into the parking lot, they saw the splendid modern addition. The Acton Congregational Church was obviously a successful parish.

In the entrance lobby, they could hear laughter from upstairs and the soft sound of paper flip-flopping out of a copy machine. Somewhere up there, the pastor was expecting them, but Mary said, "Wait, Homer, this is where it's at."

"Where what's at?" asked Homer, but he knew what she meant.

It was the bulletin board of the Acton Congregational Church. Once again, the thumbtacked notices summed up the present condition of New England Protestantism. One of them went straight to the point:

WHAT IS THE MEANING OF LIFE?

"Good question," murmured Homer, moving on to the next, which was a call to action:

ARE YOU GOING TO BE ONE OF MANY TO MAKE THE ANTIQUES
SHOW AND SALE A SUCCESS?

Another listed the dishes to be cooked for Rosie's Place:

SLOPPY JOES, COLESLAW, SHEET CAKE WITH WHITE FROSTING
(NO EXCEPTIONS, PLEASE).

"Sounds delicious," said Homer. "What's Rosie's Place anyway?"

"Oh, Rosie's Place is famous. I was there once. It's on Harrison Street, near Boston City Hospital. Nice church ladies come in from the suburbs in their Orvis sweaters and slacks from L.L. Bean. They bring the food and heat it up and serve it to homeless women. I felt kind of crummy, as a matter of fact, like a condescending Lady Bountiful, but it's an important work, Rosie's Place."

Homer murmured, "Isn't it a shame that none of those homeless women get nice catalog in the mail. Then they, too, could be arrayed like the lilies of the field."

Mary smiled ruefully and looked down at herself. "Right, in nice Eddie Bauer shirts and Lands' End pants."

"Mr. and Mrs. Kelly?" It was the pastor, looking down at them politely from the top of the stairs.

The Reverend Theodore Jones turned out to be a scholarly clergyman who knew the history of his church from its antique beginnings to the money-raising antique shows of the present, from horses and buggies to SUVs, from lined-out hymns to the youth choir for Christian pop music.

The sanctuary was warmly Victorian, with curvilinear pews facing the pulpit. Sunlight streamed through a stained-glass window, bringing to radiant life a scene from the New Testament. Another window was a miracle of delicate patterns with a glowing benediction at the bottom:

PEACE BE WITHIN THY WALLS
PROSPERITY WITHIN THY PALACES

"Prosperity," said Ted Jones, shaking his head, apologizing. "Well, it's the old problem. Christ told His disciples to sell everything, but Acton Congregational wants us all to get rich. At least it did in the old days. I guess we wouldn't have guiding principles like that anymore."

"It seems to me," said Mary kindly, "that Acton Congregational is distributing its prosperity pretty well."

"Thank you," said their guide. "We try to."

"I like these churches," said Homer as they drove away. "Sometimes their pious effusions seem a little silly, but where else, I ask you, can you find virtue all balled up in one handful?"

"Nowhere," said Mary stoutly. "Too bad Mr. Jones didn't know anything about trees, lost churches, or Oliver Wendell Holmes. Honestly, Homer, all that stuff seems more and more absurd."

"If only," said Homer, "we could talk to that old hermit lady in Nashoba, the one with the roots and berries. She's our only hope in that department—I mean the Big Tree/Lost-Church/Poetical Department. Tell you what. I'll call Joe Bold again. Maybe he'll have some idea how we can sneak up on the old lady Fay Flint."

But Joe seemed confused by Homer's phone call. "Fay?" he said. "Who's Fay?"

"You know, the old woman in the woods. You told me about her. You said she'd know everything."

"Oh, Miss Flint. Her name's not Fay; it's Julie. Where'd you get the idea her name was Fay?"

"From you." Homer was self-righteous. "You said she was Fay."

"Right, that's just what she is. I told you that. I remember now."

There was a bewildered silence until it dawned on Homer that this was a semantic problem, like the joke about the baseball players whose names were Who and What. "You meant the adjective, not the name, is that it?"

"Exactly."

Remorsefully, Homer remembered pressing his nose against Miss Flint's window and shouting "Fay?" at her like an interfering fool.

"It's not her name," he told Mary sorrowfully. "It's her character. Miss Flint is fey."

The Madman's Ax

The door to the Nashoba pizza parlor was open, but there was no one behind the counter. As they settled themselves on the twirly stools, Mary and Homer could hear raised women's voices in another room. The argument seesawed back and forth.

"It's trash. Dump it. It's all just trash."

"No, it's not. Give that back."

"Well, take it. I don't give a damn." There was a crash, followed by two simultaneous *Whoopsies.* After a pause, one voice demanded, "What's the point? Who cares about all this stuff?" And the other cried, "I do." Then the door to the other room burst open and the bitchy girl appeared. She slammed the door behind her and stamped along the counter, glowering.

Humbly, they gave their orders, and then Mary had a bright

thought. Smiling graciously at the bitchy girl, she said, "I wonder if you know your neighbor, Miss Flint? She lives in the woods behind your shop, Miss Julie Flint?"

For an instant, the girl's eyes met Mary's, then flicked away. "Oh, her."

"You do know her?" said Homer.

"Well, there's this shortcut." The bitchy girl jerked her head backward.

"Oh, you've been there? You've seen her?"

"Not me. My sister."

"Your sister? Your sister's seen her?"

"Stupid jerk, she takes orders—groceries and stuff." The microwave beeped. The bitchy girl snatched out the pizzas, dropped them on paper plates, slapped them on the counter, and disappeared.

"A shortcut!" Mary beamed at Homer. "Why don't we try the shortcut?"

But Homer wasn't listening. In the absence of the bitchy girl, he felt free to lean far over the counter to look at the wall. The NO REST ROOMS sign was bigger than ever, but someone had tacked up a few more old photographs. One was a faded aerial view.

"Look at that," said Homer. "It must have been taken from a cliff over a valley. No, not a valley, a graveyard."

Mary put on her glasses and leaned forward, too. "What's that big white spot in the middle?"

By this time, the upper half of Homer's torso lay on the counter and his bushy head was only inches away from the picture. Triumphantly, he cried, "A tree stump. By God, I think it's a tree stump." Grinning, he pulled back and plumped himself down on the stool. "Just cut down, you see? The rest is lying on the ground."

Mary whispered, "Do you think it could be—"

"Look, never mind the roots and berries lady." Homer pushed his pizza aside. "Take a look at this. I brought along an old friend." He pulled a thin book out of his pocket. The title,

Fireside Verses, was stamped in gilt letters on the limp leather cover.

Mary leaned closer. "Oh, good, Homer, Oliver Wendell Holmes. What a nice old book."

Slowly, Homer turned the pages, shaking his head at "The One-Hoss-Shay," "The Chambered Nautilus," and "The Last Leaf." Then he stopped. "Here we are. Look at this."

The poem was called "The Madman's Ax," and in that moment, as though struck by lightning, two of their queries melted into one.

The verses began with a line from Longfellow's "The Village Blacksmith," but it turned into something else at once:

> *Under the spreading chestnut-tree*
> *A vicious killer stands;*
> *He looks up at the branches free,*
> *A great ax in his hands.*
>
> *The tree flings wide its glorious crown,*
> *Its leaves the winds caress.*
> *Two hundred years the burial ground*
> *By this tree has been blessed.*
>
> *But now the madman lifts his ax*
> *To play the devil's part.*
> *The keen blade strikes and strikes again*
> *To burst that mighty heart.*
>
> *Great nature weeps, Nashoba's jewel*
> *Lies shattered on the ground,*
> *Broken, the hearts of young and old*
> *In all the country round.*
>
> *Let good men curse the vandal vile*
> *Who killed our ancient tree.*

May this foul deed afflict his soul
Till he shall cease to be.

Homer slapped the page in triumph, and together they
looked up at the photograph on the wall, the aerial view of the
giant stump in the graveyard. There it was, the tree itself, Dr.
Holmes's glorious tree, caught on a glass plate after the madman's ax had cut it down.

Only one question was left without an answer. What did
the lost church have to do with the tree and the poet and all the
other pictures on the wall of the Nashoba Pizza Parlor—the
photographs of the hot-air balloon and the nineteenth-century
faces and the twins in their bowler hats?

Where was it, the lost church? Where on the face of the
earth?

1868

"Three Billy Goats Gruff" and *A Tale of Two Cities*

"Then tell wind and fire where to stop . .   but don't tell me."

—Madame Defarge, in Charles
Dickens's *A Tale of Two Cities*

The Limb of Satan

The future of the new church looked bright. After the first service in the meetinghouse that they had built with their own hands, the congregation milled around the door in an orgy of mutual congratulation. The men of Nashoba's Second Parish shook Josiah's hand and promised to give of their treasure. The women vowed to arrange a Sabbath school.

Isabelle was proud of her father, and even Julia Gideon smiled. Five-year-old Horace was overjoyed. He leaned against his grandmother as she sat at the organ, her knees swelling the volume to its loudest for the final chords of "Sweet Saviour, Bless Us Ere We Go." When her feet stopped bouncing on the treadles, the bellows inside the organ whined down the scale and Josiah strode up the aisle to thank her.

Laughing, Eudocia stood up and bobbed a curtsey, and Horace, perceiving that the preacher had come straight out of a storybook called the Bible, trailed after Josiah as he walked back down the aisle. At the other end of the church, Horace saw Uncle Eben climb a ladder with a rope in his hand and disappear through a hole in the ceiling. Cleverly, Horace guessed that Mr. Kibbee had pulled the rope so hard that it had fallen right off the bell. And Horace was right, because in a moment the bell tonked and Uncle Eben climbed down again. When his uncle grasped the rope and pulled, Horace put his hands on it, too, and sailed joyfully up and down as the bell began to ring in earnest.

But it was time to go. Alexander spoke kindly to Isabelle, saying, "I'll be back later this afternoon to see James." Then Ida, Alexander, Eben, Eudocia, and Horace set off for home in the spring wagon. They were none too soon. Ida ran upstairs at once because Gussie was screaming at the top of her lungs. Ida's sister handed over the baby gratefully. "I'm never going to get married," said Sallie, "nor have a baby, neither."

In the kitchen, Eudocia went to work on Sunday dinner. "Horace dear," she said, handing him a bundle of spoons, knives, and forks, "you can set the table."

Horace grabbed the bundle, hurried into the dining room, and began slapping them down on the tablecloth—here a fork, there a knife, there a spoon. When the cat bounded up on the table, Horace knew at once what to do. He said, "No, no, kitty," and picked it up around the middle. At once, the cat screeched and clawed his face. Bawling, Horace tried to drop it, but its claws were hooked into his coat and he couldn't wrestle free. Spoons, knives, and forks clattered on the floor.

Eudocia came running, plucked away the cat, and consoled the weeping boy, murmuring, "It's all right, Horace dear." Horace whimpered, but soon he was thumping around on his knees, collecting scattered knives and forks.

❧

Eudocia was devoted to her grandson. Summing him up, she had a private list of Horace's virtues and faults:

1. Horace has a loving nature.
2. He has a cheerful disposition.
3. But he's a limb of Satan.

Well, "limb of Satan" was what everybody said about their little boys. "Oh, that child is a limb of Satan."

And yet it wasn't really naughtiness when Horace climbed up on the mantelpiece and all the pretty vases smashed on the floor; or when he crawled into the clock case and bent the pendulum; or when he rocked so wildly in the rocking chair that it tipped over backward and went to pieces.

Whenever Ida despaired of her only son, Eudocia said, "It's just high spirits." And therefore when Horace climbed into her lap after dinner with his favorite storybook she gathered him close and said, "I know the one you want, Horace dear."

"The billy goats," said Horace, beaming.

For the twentieth time, she read him the story of "Three Billy Goats Gruff," those good little goats who were afraid to cross the bridge because a wicked troll lived underneath. As always, Horace trembled and hid his face against his grandmother's bosom when she turned to the picture of the wicked troll, a fiend with burning eyes and sharp, tearing claws.

Then Eudocia opened a different book to another favorite, "The Three Little Pigs." This one was enlivened by a picture of the wolf. Like the troll, it had sharp claws and a terrible jaw. Horace looked at the picture and hid his face, then looked again. When Ida came downstairs with Gussie in her arms, he bounced off his grandmother's lap and ran to his mother, wanting to be picked up.

"No, no, dear," said Eudocia, but he clung to Ida's skirts and whimpered.

With the baby squirming on her shoulder and Horace clutching at her apron, Ida was distracted. When Alexander came running downstairs with his doctor's bag, she pleaded, "Oh, please, my dear, won't you take him along?"

"Oh, yes, sir, please, sir, please, please," cried Horace. He abandoned his mother's apron and tugged at his stepfather's coat.

Alexander looked down at him doubtfully. "Will you promise me, Horace, that you'll be a good boy?"

"Oh, yes, sir, yes, yes, I will," promised Horace, plunging away and reaching up to pull his coat off the hook.

Eudocia buttoned the coat close under his chin and felt in the pockets for his mittens. They were not there. "Horace, what have you done with your mittens?"

Horace laughed and shouted, "The three little kittens, they lost their mittens."

Eudocia smiled and shook her head. "Horace dear, this isn't Mother Goose. It's turned right cold out there."

"Come on, Horace," said Alexander. "Just keep your hands in your pockets. Where's Eben?"

Not until Mab was harnessed and hitched up to the wagon again did Eudocia come running out with her hands tucked into her shawl. "Alexander, you're not going to Nashoba to see James?"

"Why, yes, I am," said Alexander. "That's just where we're going."

Horace scrambled up to sit beside Eben, and Eudocia laid her hand on Alexander's arm. "You won't let him inside, will you, Alexander? Horace must not be allowed to go inside."

The Troll

The wagon rolled smoothly along the road to Nashoba. It did not rattle and bounce. High up on the seat between his stepfather and his uncle, Horace had to do his own bouncing. The seat jiggled, but no one told Horace to stop. Alexander and Eben were lost in their own thoughts, steeling themselves for the visit to James.

Mab could feel Horace's jouncing through the trembling shafts. She cocked her ears, but her pace did not slacken. She trotted along easily toward the bridge over Nashoba Brook.

The bridge. Horace had forgotten about the bridge. At once, he stopped bouncing, wrapped his short arms around his stepfather, and buried his face in Alexander's whiskers. Was there a troll under the bridge? A monster with sharp, tearing claws?

∽✦◠

The southeast corner of the town of Nashoba displayed the predicament of the two churches in a simple right-angled triangle. One side of the triangle connected Josiah Gideon's house with the unhappy church from which he had robbed the congregation. The line stretched uphill across the burial ground, where the stump of the chestnut tree stood like a memorial to the spitefulness of Horatio Biddle and the headstone of Deacon Sweetser rose like a monument to the fury of Josiah Gideon. The second side of the triangle joined Josiah's house to the robber church itself, and the third ran straight through the woods from one church to the other.

The charged geometry of the landscape was clear to Eben and Alexander as Mab pulled up at Josiah's gate. Alexander leaped down and hitched her to the gatepost. Eben jumped down, too, and reached up for Horace.

The late afternoon sky was sunny, but the air was chill. In the doorway, Josiah's daughter, Isabelle, stood waiting to welcome Alexander and Eben, but when she saw Horace, she stepped outside and closed the door behind her.

Alexander looked at Horace gravely. "You are to stay here, boy," he told him sternly. "I won't be long."

"Oh, Horace dear," said Isabelle, coming forward and smiling down at him, "the sow farrowed yesterday. Would you like to see her little pigs?" She pointed. "They're right there in the shed."

Horace stared at the distant shed. It was made of wood, just like the house of the second little pig in the story. Horace was a clever little boy, but he was still not clear where stories ended and true things began. What if the wolf was hiding under the barn? He shook his head at Isabelle and clutched Alexander's hand.

"He mustn't come in," whispered Isabelle, glancing at Eben.

Eben nodded gravely. Alexander tweaked Horace's nose, ruffled his hair, patted his shoulder, and walked inside with Isabelle.

Eben smiled at Horace, and then he said it, too: "We won't be long."

The door of the house closed behind them with a light slam. Horace looked around for something to do. He studied the gate. There was no gate in front of his grandmother's house because there was no fence. Tentatively, he wrapped his cold hands around the top rail of the gate, set one foot on the bottom rail, and pushed off with the other. The gate swung, creaking, back and forth, banging as it struck the fence post, creaking open again as he rode it out.

The house was silent. From behind it came a soft murmur that sounded like chickens. Horace liked chickens, but these were too close to the wolf, so he didn't seek them out. A big two-horse wagon rolled by, a school barge full of children. They stared at Horace. He stared back. The barge ran smoothly past the house, the children turning their heads to keep him in sight until it disappeared around the bend on the way to an outing in Concord.

Horace stepped down from the gate and sucked his cold fingers. His stepfather and Uncle Eben had been gone a long time.

While Isabelle and her mother made tea in the kitchen, Alexander watched Eben strap his new contraption on the stump of James's right arm.

"Try it, James," said Eben. "It's supposed to open and shut." But when James lifted his arm, the gadget slid sideways and drooped. "Needs to be tighter," said Eben, adjusting it. "There, try it now."

James tried it. Eben and Alexander watched him reach out to the table beside his chair and fumble at a book. When he succeeded in picking it up, Alexander murmured softly, "Good." But when James tried to turn a page with the other hook, the book slipped and fell.

"Can you pick it up?" asked Eben quietly.

James could. He picked up *A Tale of Two Cities* and dropped it on the table. Then, chuckling, he reared up from his chair and stretched out his arms as though reaching out for something else to grasp and hold.

Alexander and Eben laughed in congratulation, but when they heard the front door open, they stopped laughing and turned their heads. Isabelle ran out of the kitchen and cried out.

Horace stood in the doorway, staring in at James.

Horace Runs

Horace turned and darted out of the house.

Alexander jumped up, snatched his coat, and ran after him, calling, "Horace, wait." Eben jumped up, too, and ran after Alexander. Isabelle wrapped a shawl around her shoulders and ran after Eben. Julia stepped out the side door to look in the henhouse and the frost-ravaged garden. At the front gate, Mab whinnied, as if she, too, were calling for Horace.

"The pig shed," cried Isabelle, running that way. Eben set off down the Acton Turnpike, shouting, "Horace, come back." Alexander took a flying leap over the stone wall into the burial ground to search among the tombstones, calling, "Horace, where are you?"

But inside the house, looking out from the dining room

window, James saw Horace tumble over the back fence and
scramble into the woods on the path to Quarry Pond. James ran
into the kitchen, threw himself against the screen door, and
plunged outside.

The troll was at his back. Horace could hear the pounding of its
terrible feet. Ducking frantically under a thorny tangle of
blackberry canes that tore at his hands and stabbed at his face, he
heard the sharp claws of the troll tear them out of its way.

In the distance, Uncle Eben was shouting, "Horace, Horace,"
but the shouts died away and the snarling howls of the troll grew
louder. Horace ran faster, afraid to look back, then screamed and
fell on his knees because something burst up in his face with a
rush of wings. But it was only a bird like an enormous chicken.
Sobbing, Horace stumbled up and scampered forward, his short
legs flying.

There was an opening ahead, a piece of sunset sky and a
gleam of water. The water was a pond. Horace knew the pond
at once because there had been a picnic there last summer, and
his mother had told him not to go near the edge because the
water was so deep, and he had stood on the rocky shore with
Josh, throwing stones into the water, trying to make them skip
the way Josh's did, *once, twice, three times,* but Horace's had all
sunk.

Now, Horace took heart because he knew the way, but the
troll seemed to know the way, too, because it was thrashing
around in the woods, running sideways to head him off. Horace
despaired, understanding at once that you couldn't fool a troll.
Turning, he plunged away from the path, with the troll roaring
close at his heels, its gigantic feet trampling the forest floor, its
terrible claws snapping at branches and twigs. Glancing fearfully
back, Horace could see only the dark purple cloud that was
obliterating the setting sun. A cold wind had sprung up and all
around him the dappled splashes of sunlight were flickering out.
Scuttling through underbrush and brambles in a sudden pelting

of raindrops, Horace did not know that he was cold, only that he was afraid.

Where could he hide? Zigzagging left and right, he found a hollow place, dropped into it, and burrowed under an umbrella of overarching ferns. They trembled over his head and the rain pattered down, and Horace mistook the drumming of his heart for the pounding feet of the troll. Like a rabbit with a dog at its heels, he jumped out of the hollow and sprinted away.

Had he fooled the troll? *No, because you couldn't fool a troll.* It was still clumping along behind him in the pouring rain, smashing and crashing closer, its fiery breath sounding very near. With hot tears running down his cheeks and water streaming from his hair, Horace made a desperate lunge toward a gleam of light that appeared for an instant between the trees. It was only a flickering glimmer, disappearing and flaring up again, but to Horace it was like a candle in the window of a cottage, the cottage of a good witch who helped little boys lost in the forest, and he blundered toward it.

But it was not a cottage. Drawing closer, Horace recognized the new church in the woods, the one Uncle Eben had built with his own hands, where this very morning his grandmother had played the organ and Horace had helped to ring the bell. Now an orange light flared in the steeple, and there were welcoming jingles from the bell.

Horace floundered across the wet ground, stretching out his arms to touch the door, because he would be safe inside. Churches were holy! Too holy for trolls! The friendly door swung open, and Horace stumbled across the sill. Quickly, he slammed the door, but it flapped open again on its hinges, and at once he saw a dark shape silhouetted against the rain.

Wailing, Horace backed away. Didn't the troll hear the bell jangling in the steeple? Didn't it know that churches were forbidden to trolls? Desperately, he stared around the shadowy room, looking for a place to hide. The church was only one big chamber without cupboards or closets, but then he remembered the ladder. Yes, there it was in the corner, its rungs matted with hay. The trapdoor in the ceiling was a square of orange light.

A ladder was nothing to Horace. With the wild wind blowing into the church through the open door and the bell tingling overhead and the clawed feet of the troll booming across the new planks of the floor, Horace scampered up the ladder, rung after rung, in a shower of sparks and wisps of falling hay. Poking his head through the trapdoor, he saw a man crouched under the bell with a lighted candle in his hand.

He recognized him at once. It was the preacher—the other preacher, not Mr. Gideon—and he was setting the hay on fire.

Horatio Biddle turned around, colliding again with the infernal bell. Below him, at the top of the ladder, a small boy stood staring up at him. Horatio set the candle down on the smoldering hay and took the boy by the throat.

A Far, Far
Better Thing

James did not mean to catch the boy. He was only trying to keep him in sight, because these woods went on forever. Josiah's woodlot lay at the edge of a thousand acres of trackless forest, stretching north into Carlisle and west, all the way to Littleton.

As a boy, he had been lost in these woods himself. For an entire November day, young James had wandered in helpless circles among the trees, unable to find his way home. With darkness had come the cold, and he had crawled into a thorny tangle, terrified of wolves and creeping things. In the morning, he had seen at once which way to go, and within the hour the domed steeple of the Nashoba church had appeared above the trees and he had run all the way home to the arms of his mother and a whipping from his father. But that lost boy had been ten years old, twice the age of the boy who was running into danger now.

Like a dog herding sheep, James headed him away from Quarry Pond, then turned him in the direction of the Acton Turnpike. Reaching out with his hooks to thrust low branches out of his way, James managed to keep the boy in sight and urge him northward. Soon, young Horace would find himself in the neighborhood of the new church that was Josiah's pride and joy, and then he would no longer be lost. Yes, there it was, beyond an ugly patch of tree stumps, a rain-darkened building with a miniature steeple.

For a moment, James slowed his steps and tried to catch his breath, but when he heard the jangle of the bell and saw the blaze of light, he began to run again. Stumbling headlong into the clearing, James saw with a single glance of his one good eye that two things were horribly wrong: the boy running into the building and the man in the steeple.

James knew the man on sight. On the mild May morning in 1864 when 2nd Lt. James Jackson Shaw had embraced his new wife, Isabelle, and joined the other volunteers at the depot, this man had been there to shake his hand and say a prayer. He was the Reverend Horatio Biddle, and he was setting the steeple on fire.

James raced across the rough wet grass and threw open the church door. Looking wildly around the dark sanctuary, he saw Horace scrambling up a ladder toward a fiery opening in the ceiling. James bounded across the floor and reached up to the rungs with his iron hands. They were awkward on the ladder, but he managed to hook his way up from rung to rung. At the top, he sprang to his feet in the burning straw and flung himself at Horatio Biddle. With one hook he slashed at the staring face and with the other arm he tugged at the boy.

The Reverend Horatio Biddle shrieked and let the child go. James plucked Horace free and dropped the screaming boy down the ladder.

Horatio, too, was sobbing, but he threw himself at the ghastly apparition that was Josiah Gideon's disfigured son-in-law. The two men grappled and the wild bell rang in the steeple—the insufferable, unbearable new steeple—and the fire in the hay took hold.

> *The ministers of Sainte Guillotine are robed and ready. . . .*
> *the knitting-women count Twenty-Two. . . . The*
> *murmuring of many voices, the upturning of many faces,*
> *the pressing on of many footsteps in the outskirts of*
> *the crowd, so that it swells forward in a mass . . .*
> *Twenty-three.*
>
> —Charles Dickens, *A Tale of Two Cities*

The Nashoba Steam Fire Society

At the foot of the ladder, Horace picked himself up, bruised and sobbing. He gave one terrified upward glance at the trapdoor, but he saw only flames.

The church door banged open and shut. Horace tottered outside and made his way to the road, the wind at his back. When the sky suddenly darkened, he looked up, half-blinded by tears and by the rain in his face, and saw an enormous balloon swoop low over the treetops.

Horace had seen the balloon before. Now, gaping, he watched it droop and lift and stretch out nearly flat, with the good fairies in their bowler hats clinging to the tipping basket. And then, as the collapsing balloon blew out of sight, a wagon rattled by on the road and the rain came down in sheets.

The balloon was hurtling east. "Shouldn't have gone up today, Jack," said Jake, clutching the railing of the basket. "Too late in the year."

Jack clapped one hand on the brim of his hat. "Seemed such a nice day, Jake."

"Raining now," said Jake, as the balloon wallowed and plunged. "Coming down like pitchforks."

Then both of them cried "Whoopsie" and fell sideways in a heap.

Scrambling to his knees, Jake pointed and shouted, "Church on fire, Jack. Looky there."

"Boy down there," hollered Jack.

"Fire department," yelled Jake. "Got to tell 'em."

The balloon lifted, billowed wildly, and sagged. The burning steeple vanished. Below them in the racing, rattling wagon, Hector waved his arms and shouted, "Jesus Christ, boys."

Jack leaned out of the basket, pointed west, and shouted, "Church on fire, Hector."

Jake leaned out the other way, pointed east, and cried, "Fire engine, Hector."

Hector stared up at them with his mouth open, then lifted his whip and brought it down on the back of his old horse. In the blowing wind and drenching rain, horse and wagon plunged away in the direction of the town green.

While the squall lasted, it was a violent downpour. Jake and Jack tumbled around in the basket of the balloon, but Jake managed to crawl on hands and knees to the firebox and relight the coals, hoping to lift the drooping bag above the trees. The coals began to smolder and the rain stopped as suddenly as it had begun, but it was too late.

"Whoopsie, Jake," cried Jack as the basket scraped and caught and then wallowed free again. "We're tickling the treetops."

"Hang on," shouted Jake. "We're going down."

A moment later, the withered balloon flopped into a tangle of branches, brushed through the outermost twigs, caught on a dozen snags, and hung suspended, sagging and deflated. A pair of identical bowler hats spiraled down through the branches and splashed in identical puddles.

Lying flat on their backs in the swaying basket, Jack and Jake considered the matter philosophically.

"Time to settle down maybe, Jack."

"Guess you're right, Jake."

"Maybe get married, Jack."

"Good idea, Jake."

"Lotsa pretty girls out there, Jack. Whoopsie, the bag's on fire."

The Nashoba Steam Fire Society was a volunteer outfit, but when Hector shouted *"Whoa"* at his wheezing horse and delivered the news, the fire bell rang and the volunteers came running. In no time at all, the boys had the boiler fired up and steaming and the team hitched up and prancing. Hector, hanging on precariously, pointed straight up the Acton Turnpike.

But instead of a burning building, the fire turned out to be a flaming balloon. Undaunted, the sturdy volunteers uncoiled their hoses, aimed a stream of water straight up in the air, and put the fire out. Then, with ladders poking into the treetops, they rescued the dangling aeronauts.

Jake and Jack were drenched, but they did their civic duty. "Hey, you fellers, there's a church on fire," said Jake earnestly, picking up his bowler hat from the middle of a puddle.

"Up the road apiece," said Jack, rescuing his from another puddle.

"Probably burned to the ground by now," said Hector with a grin.

"We'll take a look," said the heroic chief of the volunteers. "Gentlemen, hop on board."

At once, the steaming machine was tearing up the road again

with Hector, Jack, and Jake bouncing on the running board. The galloping team slowed down as the firemen caught sight of the new church. All heads swiveled to the left, looking for smoke and flame, but except for the blackened steeple, the little building seemed undamaged.

"Fire's out," said Jack.

"Rain did it," said Jake.

"Gee-up," shouted the fire chief, and soon the bold volunteers were barreling along the road in the direction of a famous tavern in the town of Acton. Neither Jack nor Jake turned their heads the other way, nor did any of the gallant firefighters, to see a small boy huddled in the wet grass.

But Eben, whipping Mab into a lather and racing after the mighty engine of the Nashoba Steam Fire Society, looked not only to the left at the blackened steeple but also to the right, to the place where his small nephew was crawling out of the ditch. Horace was wet and weeping but unhurt. Eben picked him up, wrapped him in his coat, and carried him home.

Girded for
Any Horror

Horace, oh, Horace," cried Ida, enfolding him while his grandmother ran upstairs for a dry shirt and a pair of drawers.

Eben was soaking wet, too, but he ran out again into the night and jumped up on the seat of the wagon. When Mab gave him a reproachful look, he said, "Sorry, old girl," and urged her into a canter. But at once he had to pull her to a clumsy halt, because his mother was screeching at him and handing up an umbrella. The rain had stopped, but Eben took it, popped it open, and clucked at Mab, who bounced into a trot and carried him briskly back along the road to Nashoba.

On the way, he stopped to pick up his brother-in-law. Alexander had been looking for Horace all over town. Water

trickled from his whiskers and his trousers were soaked with
mud, but he laughed with delight at Eben's good news. His gig
was waiting beside Josiah's gate, and Alexander took off at once
for home.

There was no laughter in Josiah's house. When Eben reported that Horace had been found, Josiah said grimly, "Then
it's only James who is missing," and Isabelle caught at Eben's
coat and cried, "Oh, where can he be?" and her mother said
softly, "Surely he's looking for the boy."

Then Eben remembered the blackened steeple of Josiah's
church. He began to tell them, then checked himself and said,
"I found Horace on the road beside the church. Perhaps James
was there, too. I'll go back."

Isabelle snatched up her shawl, and her mother pleaded, "No,
dear, no," but Josiah said, "Let her go."

Then Eben gave Josiah a warning look. "I'm afraid, sir, there
was a fire."

At this, Josiah pulled on his rain-drenched coat and girded
himself for any horror.

In the wagon, no one said a word as Mab trotted solemnly
along the Acton Turnpike. Nor did they speak as they stood together on the trampled grass and gazed up at the blackened
steeple in the light of Josiah's lantern. Around them, the
haunted clearing gave off a sense of sorrow. There was an ugly
smell of burning.

"Wait here," said Eben to Isabelle.

"Yes, my dear, wait," said Josiah.

"No, no," cried Isabelle, and she clung to her father's arm.

But when Eben urged her again, saying, "You must wait, Isabelle," she let go of Josiah's arm and stood back, trembling.

Waiting alone in the dark, she listened to the hollow echo of
their boots on the floorboards inside the church. Then there
were other small noises, and finally no sound at all. Eben and
Josiah had been gone a long while when Isabelle at last called
out, "Father?"

There was no reply, but soon Josiah's lantern flickered in the doorway and he came out, followed by Eben. Their faces were grave.

Josiah went to his daughter and took her hand. "Oh, what is it?" whispered Isabelle. When he told her that they had found James and that he was dead, she broke down and fell to her knees.

Isabelle did not often weep. She had cared for her stricken husband in hospitals in Washington and Philadelphia and in a rooming house in New York City, and here at home she had nursed him with unfailing devotion. For three suffering years, she had borne it without faltering, but now she threw herself down on the wet ground. Her sobs were not gentle and lady-like. Isabelle blubbered and tore with her fingers at the grass.

Her father murmured in pity and stooped to help her, but Eben reached past him, lifted Isabelle in his arms, and carried her to the wagon. Then Josiah took the reins and Eben kept his arm around Isabelle, who leaned against him, racked with weeping.

NOW

The Lost and Found Steeple

❧❧

TODAY'S SPECIALS
Green Pepper, Onion & Mushroom Pizza
Provolone & Pepperoni Pizza
Cheese, Pepperoni & Sausage Pizza
Mozzarella & Pepperoni Pizza
Tomato, Sausage & Zucchini Pizza
The Works

The Call of Nature

For the customers of the Nashoba pizza parlor, the lack of public rest rooms was like the scarcity of indoor plumbing in the old town of Nashoba. Mary whirled the car into the weedy parking lot and zoomed to a stop, and Homer leaped out and plunged into the wilderness.

It was not a pretty wilderness, but a wasteland. Homer shoved hastily through a thicket of burdock, collecting burrs on the sleeves of his sweater, and headed for a stand of dead trees. But even here the protective cover was too sparse for Homer's modesty, which was more hoity-toity than one might have expected in a burly, bewhiskered male of the species, six feet, six inches tall. Homer pushed on and broke through the wasteland at last into a glade screened by willow trees. It was perfect.

Homer relieved himself gratefully, then looked around as he zipped up his pants, aware of something odd about the place, a kind of frowsy dignity.

Then he saw the reason. A tall stone stood at one side of the glade, half-overgrown with Virginia creeper. It did not look like a glacial boulder. Ankle-deep in brambles, Homer pulled aside the crimson leaves. He was not surprised to find an inscription neatly carved on the face of the granite. The letters were encrusted with moss and lichen, but he could make out a pair of crossed swords, the mark of a soldier's grave.

Back in the parking lot, he found Mary napping in the backseat. "Come on," he said, giving her a shake. "You've got to see this."

She reared up sleepily and said, "Do I have to?"

"Yes, you have to."

Grumpily, she waded after him through the burdock and the dead trees. Homer lifted aside the trailing curtains of willow and led her into the glade. Then she, too, was entranced by the gravestone. She fumbled for her glasses and peered at the inscription. "Lieutenant," she murmured. "Lieutenant somebody. Wait a sec. I have it—'Lieutenant James Jackson Shaw.' That's what it says."

"Strange, don't you think? A soldier buried here all by himself?"

Homer's instinctive nosiness was fully aroused. On the way back to the parking lot, he jerked open the door of a shed attached to the back of the pizza parlor and poked around inside. When Mary pulled firmly on his shirttail, he said, "No, no, wait." Reaching past a spade with a broken handle and a snaggletoothed rake, he murmured, "My God."

It was a masterpiece. Behind the broken tools stood a piece of upright furniture carved with fruit and flowers. A noble pair of robed and bearded men supported a classical pediment.

Mary whispered, "What is it?" and Homer said, "Why is it here?"

Dreamily, they walked around the building and opened the door of Nashoba Pizza, hoping the girl behind the counter would stop being bitchy long enough to tell them about the gravestone and the beautiful object in the shed.

"Oh, hi, there," she said with a radiant smile. "What can I do for you this fine morning? Did you ever see such a day? Sunshine and blue sky? All's well with the world." The girl laughed. "More or less, I guess."

They gaped at her. What had happened to her bitchiness? Had there been a religious conversion? A flash of revelation?

"Oh, the usual, I guess," said Mary, sitting down on a stool and glancing doubtfully at Homer.

"Right, the usual," said Homer. "Me, too."

"I'm sorry," said the no-longer-bitchy girl, "but I don't know what you usually order." She laughed again. "Oh, it was my sister. You must have been ordering from my sister, Jane."

"No, no, it was you," said Homer, dumbfounded.

"Yes, it certainly was," said Mary. But then her head cleared. "You mean you and your sister are—"

"Twins. She's Jane Spratt; I'm Jean." Jean smiled and nodded at the oddly shaped cupboard that rose high against the wall behind the counter. They had noticed it before. It was bedecked with little shelves, a tiny mirror, and a host of frolicsome curlicues. Jean reached behind a bottle of catsup and extracted a picture. "You see? It runs in the family."

They had seen this, too, the faded photograph of two identical men in bowler hats standing with arms akimbo in front of a hot-air balloon.

In Homer's cross-eyed vision, everything began to double. There were two bowler hats, two bottles of catsup, two identical young women. "You mean they were twins just like you?

Mary, too, was dazzled. "You mean twins run in the family?"

"Right." Jean looked fondly at the photograph. "One of these guys was our great-great-great-grandfather, only we don't know which. Now tell me"—Jean lifted a lid of the cupboard, revealing a keyboard, then pumped a pedal with one foot and ran her fingers up and down the yellow keys—"what is your usual, exactly?"

The Darkroom

I t was a church once, you see," said Jean, whirling around and waving her arms. "This whole building, it was a church."

"A church!"

"Of course it was." Jean turned back to the keyboard, pumped a pedal again, and played a chord. "This was the organ, you see, and this must have been some kind of signboard." She reached up and pulled down the thumbtacked menu. "You know, on the front door."

The wooden board that had been hidden under the list of pizzas was adorned with a tree carved in magnificent low relief.

"It's the tree," gasped Homer. "I'll bet it's the chestnut tree in the poem, the one that was cut down." Rearing up from his stool, he leaned over the counter and pointed at the aerial photograph on the wall. "See there, see that stump?"

Mary was stunned, too, but she failed to see the connection. "The carved tree isn't a stump, Homer; it's a big and beautiful tree. It could be any old tree." She turned to Jean, bewildered. "Do you know what the carving had to do with this place when it was a church?"

"I don't know, but it was right there on the old door, before we turned the place into a pizza parlor. Jane and me, we did it. I mean we had to, because our parents didn't leave us anything except the apartment in town and this place. We could see that it was a really great location, right here on Two A, a perfect place for customers. So me and Jane, we got a bank loan and hired a bunch of carpenters and ordered stuff from a restaurant-supply place, and—*presto*—we were in business." Jean tucked her thumbs into the straps of her apron and waggled her fingers proudly. "But like, hey, you know what?"

Mary smiled and said, "What?"

"Before we lived here—I mean way back in the old days—it was a business place then, too, sort of a studio for taking pictures, I mean after it was a church. At least that's what our dad thought. Want to see? Oh, wait a sec." Jean ran around the counter and turned the sign on the door from OPEN to CLOSED. "Okay, come look."

Obediently, they followed her through the door behind the counter and found themselves in a large room with pointed windows along two sides.

Homer looked at Mary and they shook their heads, ashamed of their own blindness. How could they have missed it? They had noticed only the storefront with its flickering sign, NASHOBA PIZZA. And just now, transfixed by the mysterious object in the shed, they had paid no attention to the pointed shapes of the windows.

"This was the sanctuary, I guess you'd call it," said Jean. "See the pews?"

"Pews, oh, right," mumbled Homer, staring at the rows of benches. Sunlight from the clear glass of the windows streaked across them, and there were splashes of red and blue from the stained glass at the top.

"My grandfather and his brother grew up here," said Jean. "They were twins, too. My father wasn't a twin, he was an only son, so the place was all his. He really cared about it, so after we grew up here and Mom died, he did his best to put everything back the way it must have been when it was a church. He moved us into the apartment in town, and then he began tearing down rickety walls and clearing out all the furniture and even the kitchen stove and refrigerator. He got rid of everything and tried to make it look like a church again. My sister, she thought it was crazy, but I sort of liked it."

"Well, of course," said Homer, smiling at her and looking around. "So do we."

An important question was still unanswered. "But Jean," protested Mary, "why did it stop being a church in the first place?"

"I haven't a clue. But look, follow me. There's something else."

Jean led them to the far end of the sanctuary and pulled aside a curtain. "See? It's sort of a darkroom."

"A darkroom!"

"My sister, she wants me to throw all this stuff out. But my father really cared about it." The space behind the curtain was full of blocky objects. Jean edged past them and pulled up a roller shade. "See, this big camera is on some funny kind of tri-pod."

"A cantilever, I think," murmured Homer.

"What on earth is this?" asked Mary, running her hands over a tall stand that looked like a coatrack.

"Oh, I figured that one out," said Jean. "In the old days, when the exposures were longer than they are now, this thing stood behind you to keep your head still."

For a moment, they looked around and said nothing. Jean picked up a dusty pamphlet and handed it to Homer, and he began reading it aloud. " 'Jack and Jacob Spratt, Aerial and Portrait Photographers.' " Then he stopped and looked at Jean. "Your ancestors? The twins in the picture? They had a camera in their balloon?"

Jean was fascinated. "Oh, that's fabulous. I'll bet they did."

"They could have aimed it over the side," said Mary.

"With the cantilever contraption," said Homer happily. "Clever, that's what they were, your ancestors."

"And brave, too," said Mary graciously.

"Well, yes, I guess they were," said Jean, "doing all that stuff way up in the sky. Oh, wait a sec." Jean looked at her watch and said, "Whoopsie, I've got to go. I'm supposed to be someplace else."

She pulled aside the curtain and ran out of the darkroom. Homer and Mary hurried after her down the center aisle of the long-lost church and through the far door into the pizza parlor. "I've got to deliver these," said Jean, reaching under the counter and picking up a couple of grocery bags.

Nothing could astonish Mary now. "Jean Spratt's Delivery Service?"

"No, no, it's just one old woman, Julie Flint, up the hill. She doesn't get out much, so sometimes she gives me a list and then I get the stuff. There's a shortcut to her place through the woods."

"Julie Flint?" Homer was staggered. "You mean the Miss Flint who is—"

He had almost said "the roots and berries woman," but Mary interrupted quickly. "I gather Miss Flint is something of a recluse?"

"Well, I guess you could call her that, but she doesn't hide away from me. Julie and me, we're good old pals."

"Pals," echoed Homer. "Oh, please, dear Jean, may we come, too?"

Julie Flint

The path was a narrow, winding track, but Jean Spratt's feet had long since beaten it down. Mary and Homer followed as Jean made her way to the home of Julie Flint, Homer's witch in the woods, the old recluse who was not, after all, a gatherer of nuts and berries.

Carrying her bags of groceries, Jean moved in front of them through a field of wildflowers, where doilies of Queen Anne's lace lay on the grass like delicate washing. When Mary poked him, Homer said, "Oh, right," and took the bags from Jean.

The path was indeed a shortcut. Soon, Homer recognized the fence around Miss Flint's vegetable garden and, beyond it, the roof of her house.

"Wait here," said Jean. "She's a little shy. Last month, some strange man banged on her door, pushed his face against the window, and called her by the wrong name. Some rude barbarian."

Mary suppressed a laugh and Homer flinched. Humbly, he put the grocery bags back in Jean's arms without a word. Silently, they watched her set off for Miss Flint's door. It opened at her knock and Jean disappeared inside. They waited, leaning over the fence to admire the sprawling zucchini and squash vines, the clusters of green peppers, and the tepees thickly hung with tomatoes. "Nice garden," murmured Mary.

"No weeds here," said Homer. "Not like our patch."

Mary looked at him and said tartly, "I suppose you think it's my fault?"

Homer thought carefully. "Yes, I think it's your fault. It's also my fault and your sister's fault and the selectmen's fault. In fact, it's the fault of everybody in Middlesex County who failed to weed our tomato patch."

Mary laughed and said, "Sorry" just as Jean Spratt looked out the door of Miss Flint's house and gave them a welcoming wave. At once, Mary took Homer's arm and whispered, "Now remember, Homer, you mustn't loom."

"Loom? What do you mean, 'loom'?"

"You're just so big and overwhelming. Try to shrink down a little."

Obediently, Homer hunched his shoulders, and they walked into the enchanted cottage of the good witch of the woods.

Indoors, the air was moist with steam. Like a proper witch, Miss Flint was hovering over a boiling caldron, but she was only canning tomatoes. For an instant, she glanced up, then looked back at her task. Reaching into the kettle with a pair of tongs, she lifted out a steaming jar, thumped it down on a towel, and reached into the pot for another. Miss Flint's back was hunched and bowed, her face was an intricate complex of wrinkles, and one eye was blank and blind.

They were afraid to speak, but Jean said boldly, "Mr. and Mrs. Kelly are here to see you, Julie."

"Well, fine," said Julie Flint, leaning over her sterilizing kettle. "But they'll just have to wait a sec."

They stood back patiently and watched her lift four more scalding jars out of the pot. At last, she said, "Okay, all done," switched off the stove, and turned around slowly. She smiled at Mary, then scowled at Homer with a sharp glance of recognition. "You were here before."

"Yes," mumbled Homer. "I'm sorry, Miss Flint. I didn't mean to be rude."

"Well, you were." Miss Flint waved at a circle of wicker chairs and said, not ungraciously, "Why don't you sit down?"

They obeyed. Then, while Jean helped with the putting away of the groceries, they studied the furnishings of Miss Flint's house. Everything was shipshape—the tables and chairs, the bookshelves, the cupboards, and the forest of potted plants. Only a desk under the window was messy with books and papers. They stared at it greedily.

"Now," said Miss Flint, lowering herself carefully into a wicker chair lined with pillows, "what is it you want?"

They looked at each other. How should they begin? But Jean Spratt was leaving. She touched Miss Flint's shoulder and said, "Do you have another list for me, Julie?"

"No, my dear, thank you. Did you take what I owe you from the coffee can?"

"Fifteen dollars and thirty cents, and I left the receipt." With a wave at Mary and Homer, Jean slipped out the door and shut it gently behind her.

It was brass-tack time. Homer hitched himself forward in his chair and said bravely, "You see, Miss Flint, I was told by our friend Joe Bold that you know more about the history of Nashoba than anyone else."

"Yes, Miss Flint," said Mary. "You see, we're studying local churches."

"I'm working on a book, you see, Miss Flint," said Homer.

"It's a sequel, you see," said Mary. "I mean, there was another book before."

"You don't mean—not *Hen and Chicks?*" Julie Flint pulled herself out of her chair and stood up. "Sir, do you mean to say that you wrote *Hen and Chicks?*"

Mary looked at Homer fearfully, and he cowered. "Well, yes, Miss Flint, I'm afraid I did."

But then she was seizing his hand and shaking it. "Congratulations, Homer Kelly. That's what I call a good book."

"You mean"—Homer couldn't believe it—"you actually read it?"

"Of course I read it. Fascinating stuff. It should've been a bestseller."

"Well, actually," simpered Homer, "it was a bestseller, only you're the only person who seems to have read it."

It was a breakthrough. Suddenly, the windows brightened with bursts of afternoon sunshine as Miss Flint opened wide the gates of her memory. She told them stories about her early life, about her mother, Elizabeth, and her father, Ebenezer; her brother, Henry, and his foolish son, Cosimo; and about Cosimo's even more foolish son, Howard.

"Howard?" said Mary. "You don't mean Howard Flint?" She gasped and looked at Homer, who laughed and slapped his knee. "You see, Miss Flint," said Mary, "my sister and I must be related to you. At least we're related to Howard Flint. He's our second cousin three times removed, or perhaps our third cousin twice removed—we never could figure out which. Homer and I ran into him last year."

"You're related to Howard?" said Julie Flint. "Well, I'm sorry for you. The boy's an ass."

"We noticed that," said Homer, "but never mind Howard. Please, Miss Flint, could you go further back? I mean way, way back?"

"Well, certainly, but before we leave the subject of my great-nephew," said Miss Flint acidly, "you might be interested to know that he burned down my house."

"He what?" Homer was aghast.

"Howie Flint?" said Mary. "He burned down your house?"

"The fool." Julie's anger was mixed with scorn. "I was born in that house, and so were my father and grandmother. It meant the world to me. It stood right there on the green, across from the burial ground. Then in a few awful minutes, it was gone. Before the roof came down, I managed to rescue some of my precious papers and pictures. Luckily, the firefighters didn't see me running back inside, because they were trying to save the barn. But they were scandalized when I came running out with my pajamas on fire."

"Oh, Miss Flint," said Mary faintly.

"But how did it happen?" asked Homer. "Why on earth did Howie burn down your house?"

"Mad at me, I guess," growled Julie.

"Mad at you!"

"Ten years ago, I invited poor orphaned Howie to share Thanksgiving with me. Well, it was a painful family duty. But that night, I found him stealing money from my desk drawer. When I bawled him out, he gave it back and sobbed and said he was sorry, but then during the night he started the fire and skedaddled, although I don't suppose that's a current expression." Julie smiled grimly. "So doing a favor for a tiresome young relative turned out to be even more painful than I'd thought."

Mary was indignant. "You mean he got away with it?"

"Clean away."

"What a horrible man," said Mary angrily. "He stole things from us, too. I mean from my sister and me."

"Listen here, Miss Flint," said Homer. "We just happen to know where Howard Flint can be found. He could be arrested and punished. He's a menace to the human race."

"Oh, never mind. The house was gone, but I sold the land for a goodly sum, and there's a jerry-built mansion on it now. Then I built this place on a piece of land I'd inherited. It was the remains of my great-grandfather's woodlot. Well, say now!" Julie grinned at them. "I should tell you about my great-grandfather.

For thirty-five years, Josiah Gideon was pastor of the parish church, the one on the green."

"The church on the green," repeated Homer reverently. "You mean Joe Bold's church, the one everybody calls Old West?"

"Tell us about it," whispered Mary. "Oh please, Miss Flint."

"Now look here, you two, why don't you call me Julie?" The old woman unhooked a cane from the back of her chair and hobbled across the room to her disordered desk. For a moment, she shuffled among the books and papers, then pulled out one of the books. "Some of it's pretty sad," she said, glancing at Mary with one keen eye while the other stared blankly at nothing. "This is the medical record of Civil War cases handled by the surgeons who cared for my grandmother's first husband, Lieutenant James Shaw."

Homer was quick to speak up. "We saw his tombstone, Miss Flint," he said, but Mary murmured, "Wait, Homer, let her finish."

"It's a medical textbook," said Julie, handing the book to Homer. "Terrible pictures. Don't look at it now. Take it home."

Homer took the book and said, "Miss Flint, can you tell us anything about the history of Jean's little restaurant? Back in the old days, when it was a church?"

"Oh, you figured that out, did you?" said Julie, her old eyes glittering. "Yes, indeed I can. How much time have you got?"

She talked and talked. Laboriously, she shuffled back and forth across the room to fish among the papers on her desk and snatch out photograph albums and newspapers and folders. She went on and on, as though she had been waiting for years to tell the story of Nashoba's Second Parish, and the small church with a homely steeple that had been built by her grandfather Eben and great-grandfather Josiah and all the rest of an obstreperous congregation of men and women intent on raising from the dead an illustrious fallen tree.

The Stump in
the Graveyard

There was a sign at the gate: NASHOBA MUNICIPAL CEMETERY. The Reverend Joseph Bold walked down the hill with Mary and Homer Kelly to the foot of the burial ground, where a stone wall meandered along Quarry Pond Road.

"It's somewhere in this clump of trees," said Joe. He led them ducking through a small forest of bushy saplings to an opening in the center, where a circle of small stumps surrounded a moss-grown giant like chairs around a table.

"It was huge all right," said Joe. He took a tape measure out of his coat, stretched it across the stump, whistled, snapped the tape shut, and said, "Eight feet, four inches."

As they fumbled their way out again, Homer said learnedly, "I've been reading about chestnut trees. The roots keep sending

up shoots, but they don't last long. Ever since 1904, when the
blight appeared, every chestnut tree in the country has been
doomed to an early death."

"Just like James Thurber's aunt." Joe laughed and mopped at
his eye, which had been scraped by a whippy twig. "If I remember correctly, she was the only human being who ever died
of the chestnut blight."

"But it wasn't the blight that destroyed this tree," said Mary.
"Miss Flint told us about it. It was cut down in 1868."

"By order of your predecessor in the pulpit," said Homer,
prodding Joe's shirt with an accusing finger. "One Horatio Biddle. Act of vandalism."

Joe held up protesting hands. "Don't blame me. It was long
before my time. Now, if you two will excuse me, I've got an ap-
pointment with an engaged couple."

Mary smiled. "You're going to lecture them about their
marriage vows?"

"On the contrary—they'll lecture me. They'll want a service
expressing their innermost convictions." Joe said good-bye and
ambled away, mumbling, "Big chunks of the *Rubaiyat,* I'll bet.
'A jug of wine,' et cetera."

Mary and Homer were in no hurry. The graveyard looked
like a gold mine. For the rest of the afternoon, they wandered
up the hill and down again, reading tombstones. Surely some of
the dramatis personae in Julie Flint's stories and recollections
and miniature biographies lay buried right here beneath their
feet.

They began with the impressive tombstone at the top of the
hill. "Deacon Samuel Sweetser," said Mary, reading the inscription. "It looks older than the rest."

Deacon Sweetser's monument dwarfed the small stone beside it:

THE REVEREND HORATIO BIDDLE

1820–1868

Pastor

FIRST PARISH OF NASHOBA

1851–1868

Mary frowned. "Wasn't he—"

"You bet he was." Homer made a kicking motion at Biddle's tombstone, but he stopped his big shoe before it struck. "Horatio Biddle, he's the vandal vile, remember? The one who gave the order for the felling of the chestnut tree."

"Oh, ugh," said Mary, moving on.

Halfway down the sloping burial ground, they found the splendid memorial to the next pastor of Nashoba's First Parish:

THE REVEREND JOSIAH GIDEON

✳

1823–1903

Cherished Pastor

FIRST PARISH OF NASHOBA

1868–1903

and

His Beloved Wife,

JULIA LORD GIDEON

1828–1908

"Julie's great-grandparents," said Homer. "And this one marks the grave of her grandfather."

EBEN BARTHOLOMEW FLINT
1847–1928
Pvt., 2nd Maryland
Volunteer Infantry, 1863
Architect, Deacon,
Selectman,
Moderator of Town Meeting

❧

Let us now praise famous men,
And our fathers that begat us.
All these were honoured
in their generations,
and were the glory in their times.

"Eben Bartholomew Flint," said Mary. "Remember him, Homer?" He was Ida's younger brother. Did Eben have a wife?"

"Well, of course he must have been married," said Homer, "if Julie's his granddaughter. Look, we've got to go."

But on the way back up the hill, they were attracted by the inscription on another stone. "Look, Homer," cried Mary, "here are Jean's ancestors, the Spratt brothers."

Homer laughed, remembering the twins in their bowler hats. "Not only were they born at the same time, but they died in the same year."

"Maybe it was a joint decision."

"Or perhaps they were called home at the same instant by the dear ones who had gone before."

"Or it could have been a scientific miracle of molecular sympathy. You know, a simultaneous decay of protoplasm."

"Well, whatever."

Here Lie the Mortal Remains of
Two Brothers
JOHN AND JACOB SPRATT
Portrait and Aerial Photographers
1843–1913

❧

May their souls fly to heaven
As their bodies flew on earth.

The Forbidden Book

It was Homer's turn to take the wheel. On the way home, Mary reached between her knees into the bag of books that had been loaned to them by Julie Flint.

"Oh, I remember this one," said Mary, laughing. "There's a whole shelf of Tom Speedy books in my sister's house; they were written by our great-grandfather."

"My God." Homer pulled the car to a stop on the shoulder of the road and leaned sideways to gaze in wonder at *Tom Speedy's Aeroplane.* "Do you mean to tell me Horace Morgan was your great-grandfather?"

"Of course he was. Didn't you know that?"

"I did not." Homer was ecstatic. "If I'd known you were Horace Morgan's great-granddaughter, I'd have fallen to my knees right way. They were such great stories—*Tom Speedy and His Motorcar, Tom Speedy and His Locomotive, Tom Speedy and His Hot-Air Balloon.* Well, I suppose nobody reads them anymore, but I had a passion for them when I was ten."

At home, they went straight to the kitchen. Homer opened two bottles of beer and Mary sliced tomatoes and cucumbers from their garden patch and dumped them in the food processor. As the machine whirled them noisily around, she shouted a question at Homer. "Why do you think she retired from the world?"

"Julie Flint?" Homer looked down at his empty bowl. When Mary turned off the noisy machine, the clock ticked in the silent kitchen. She poured the gazpacho into the bowls and sat down, and at last Homer said solemnly, "Because she's not wearing rose-colored glasses."

"Well, neither are we."

"Oh yes we are." Homer picked up his spoon. "Everybody who isn't a recluse or a suicide wears rose-colored glasses. That includes you and me. We have to look through some kind of distorting lens, because if we got a really good look at the various miseries in the world, we wouldn't be able to carry on from day to day."

After lunch, they carried the bag of Julie's books into the front room. Mary took out the forbidden book and set it on the coffee table. It was an oversize clothbound volume, its black cover stamped with gold. She looked at it fearfully. "Julie said to open it with care."

"Well, go ahead."

"I'm afraid of it. It's full of terrible pictures, she said."

"Well, I'm not afraid; I'm curious."

"Okay, you look at it then."

Homer reached for the book, opened it, and turned the pages slowly. Screwing up her courage, Mary said, "Okay, show me."

"No," said Homer, and he slammed the book shut.

"Homer dear, I happen to be a grown woman."

"Of course you are. Forgive me." He opened the book again and they looked at it together.

It was an atlas of Civil War injuries photographed *"by order of the surgeon general."* Some of the pictures were of gangrenous limbs before amputation; some showed the postoperative stumps, others the odd shapes of resectioned arms and legs. The most harrowing were photographs of facial disfigurements—missing lower jaws and noses, drooping, sightless eyes, mouths hideously crimped to one side. Among them were studies of heroic attempts at surgical repair.

The last page described the case of Lt. James Jackson Shaw. Mary made pitying noises. James was blind in one eye. The bridge of his nose was gone and part of his lower jaw. His arms were stumps. Below the photograph was his medical history.

Homer and Mary read the surgeon's dry report.

2nd Lt. James Jackson Shaw, 32nd Massachusetts Volunteer Infantry. Severely wounded, April 1, 1865, at Five Forks, Virginia, in one of the last engagements of the late war.

His wounds resulted from the premature explosion of a shell as it was rammed home in the muzzle of a twelve-pounder Napoléon. His injuries were multiple. The humors of the right eye were evacuated, the nasal bones fractured, and a portion of the inferior maxilla carried away, resulting in great deformity and loss of speech.

Worse still was the catastrophic destruction of both hands. Within an hour of the explosion, amputations were performed in a field hospital. Both arms were removed at the wrist. The wounds cicatrized well and the patient was transferred to St. Joseph's Hospital in New York City, where portions of exfoliated bone were removed and the first of four facial operations performed by Dr. Gordon Buck. Over a two-year period, there were three other attempts at repair with successive skin grafts.

Homer closed the book. When he could speak, he said, "Well, it's war. It's any war. Even now, the worst casualties are spirited away somewhere. Nobody's allowed to photograph men as damaged as this. Why, dear me, it would be in such poor taste. So the poor guys spend the rest of their lives hidden away in veterans' hospitals. Their fellow citizens hear the statistics—you know, how many men were killed and how many wounded—but they never see the worst that can happen to the young men they so blithely send off to war. Otherwise, they might refuse to send them."

"But sometimes we have to send them," murmured Mary.

"Only when the particular war we send them to is chosen pretty damn carefully," growled Homer.

A Bad Day
for Homer

Sometimes, Mary Kelly imagined going back in time to the moment when she and Homer had first met. What if they could relive that crucial encounter? Given a second chance, would Homer murmur, "Excuse me" and turn his back? Would she?

Poor Old Homer, his new book was done, hurried to a finish. At the last minute, he had added an exciting new chapter about the lost and found church in the town of Nashoba, and then he had rushed the manuscript to his editor by overnight mail.

Next day, Luther called to say, "Well, it's about time, Homer. Your last bestseller has slipped right off the bottom of the list, but now, please God, you'll be back on top again."

But the publishing world proved fickle. Luther called a few months later to say regretfully, "Sorry, Homer, but this one's a dud, I'm afraid. We fired off a couple hundred review copies, but nobody took the bait."

Mary took him out on the river to cheer him up, but it didn't work. "It's not just the new one that's failing," said Homer gloomily, dipping his paddle in rosy pieces of reflected sky. "Luther says *Hen and Chicks* is going out of print."

Mary changed the subject. "Look, Homer, it's that time of day again. Thoreau's favorite time."

"What time do you mean?" groaned Homer.

"When the setting sun and the rising moon are equal and you can't tell whether it's day or night."

"Who the hell cares?" Homer had said the same thing before, laughing in triumph. This time, he said it bitterly, not bothering to look east or west.

Fortunately, the celestial bodies themselves seemed to care. The sun went down in a fiery display of pink and crimson cloud and the moon rose slowly over Fairhaven Bay, majestic and serene, oblivious of human trouble, of books and disappointments, of churches and scandals and the miscellaneous sufferings of mortal flesh.

Homer's *Steeplechase* had failed, but the steeples themselves remained, parish churches all across the face of New England, with their Bible Sundays, knitting ministries, bicycle rides for hunger, Easter luncheons, globalization studies, intergenerational potlucks, and even their occasional hanging sermons. There they stood on a thousand village greens, wooden structures as simple as barns and as commonplace as gas stations, but of a timeless and surpassing beauty.

1868

Three Trees

I had a little nut tree, nothing would it bear
But a silver nutmeg and a golden pear;
The king of Spain's daughter came to visit me,
And all for the sake of my little nut tree.

—Anonymous, nursery rhyme

A Miscellaneous
Harvest

The first of the three trees had been real, but it was gone
now, leaving only an enormous stump in a thicket of
sprouted saplings at the foot of the burial ground. The second
was the tree of Mr. Darwin, but it existed only in the head of
Josiah Gideon. The third was also invisible, but, like a grafted
tree in an orchard, it bore a miscellaneous harvest: *The Origin of
Species* and the *Book of Genesis*, *The Autocrat of the Breakfast Table*,
Caesar's *Gallic Wars* and *Jack and the Beanstalk*, *A Tale of Two
Cities* and *Three Billy Goats Gruff*, Cicero's *Orations* and Miss
Fuller's *Woman in the Nineteenth Century*.

Surely some of the crucial events of the year 1868 in the
town of Nashoba were the fruit of this latter tree. Perhaps they
had been read into being.

It was late September in New England. Noisy flocks of wild geese flapped down on Quarry Pond and took off again, heading south. The gossamer egg sacs of spiders appeared in the corners of rooms. Cattle were driven to Brighton and apples carted to Boston. Pumpkins swelled in the fields and curtains of wild grapes hung on stone walls. Virginia creeper and poison ivy blazed on dead trees. Wood was corded, coal got in.

In Nashoba, there were funeral services in both churches. A lawsuit was dropped, and Josiah Gideon hired a firm of carpenters to repair his half-burned steeple.

But how does a five-year-old boy recover? In the house of Eudocia Flint, Horace did not speak. Night after night, he woke up screaming. Ida and Alexander took him into their bed, and in the morning he climbed into his grandmother's lap. All during that anxious week, he spoke only once—when Eudocia brought out the storybook. "No," said Horace, pushing it away.

Nursery rhymes were safer, although Mother Goose sometimes reveled in dire events, like the fate of the three blind mice and the fall of Humpty-Dumpty. But the cat and the fiddle were harmless, and Horace smiled at the cow that jumped over the moon. He liked the blackbirds popping out of the pie and the fine lady with rings on her fingers and bells on her toes. And when Eudocia told him stories about his own toes—"This little piggy went to market"—Horace laughed out loud.

In Nashoba, there were important changes. The Prudential Committee of the First Parish Church returned to its duty and chose Josiah Gideon as its new pastor. Then, since the newly built church was no longer needed, Josiah and his friends offered it for sale.

But who would be interested in an empty church? Through the rest of the fall and all winter and spring, it stood empty. The door blew open, dead leaves piled up in the corners, and bats hung from the rafters. In June, at long last, the property was acquired by two pairs of newlyweds. And before long, to everyone's surprise, a new enterprise appeared on the Acton Turnpike: a photographic studio à la mode. At once, it began doing a land-office business in cartes de visite, cabinet photographs, and touching images of deceased infants.

As for Ingeborg Biddle, she dawdled and delayed. Although the returning congregation lost no time in calling Josiah Gideon to the pulpit of the First Parish Church, Ingeborg was in no rush to vacate the parsonage. There were too many important things to do, such as the removal of her bathroom fixtures.

"What do you want we should do with them?" asked the plumber after wrenching free all the connections.

"Bury them," said Ingeborg, having vowed that no member of the Gideon family would ever enjoy their splendor.

"Well, all right, missus," said the plumber, "if you say so." But he wisely took them home to glorify his own domestic arrangements, while Ingeborg moved to Cambridge with the rest of her worldly goods.

On the whole, she was not sorry to leave Nashoba. For one thing, she had no intention of being whispered about as *poor Widow Biddle, whose late husband—here, dear, I'll whisper it in your ear.* For another, she was tired of country smells, country noises, and country society. Her new friends in Cambridge were so much more sophisticated. Soon, Ingeborg established a new series of *conversaziones.* From the start, they were more successful than her pitiful afternoons among the provincial ladies of Nashoba.

When the parsonage was empty at last, Josiah and Julia moved in, leaving their widowed daughter, Isabelle, in possession of the house at the corner of Quarry Pond Road and the Acton Turnpike.

A year later, Eben Flint bought the house from his new father-in-law. On the night of their wedding, Eben fell on his knees before Isabelle. She knelt, too, and wrapped him in her loose long hair. Not until noon of the next day did they rouse themselves because sunlight was falling through the window at a scandalous angle. The sun was so high above the town of Nashoba that even the tall tombstone of Deacon Sweetser in the burial ground cast no shadow, nor did the stone soldier on his pedestal, nor even the steeple of the First Parish Church.

Within the year, Isabelle gave birth to a baby boy. Eventually, five children—Bartholomew, William, Eudocia, Julia, and Ebenezer—made the house ring with the noise of their games and their laughter and their fighting.

Eben set up his drafting table in the room where James had spent the last summer of his life. His architectural practice went well, but sometimes he had to rear up out of his chair and shout, "Pipe down," although it didn't do much of any good.

As time went by, Eben often thought about Isabelle's first husband, whose place he had taken. Sometimes he told himself that there was a sort of poetical connection between the chestnut tree and James Jackson Shaw. Perhaps by his heroic action the lopped man had been made whole, just as the lopped and fallen tree had been born again. Sometimes Eben believed in this noble parallel, and sometimes he didn't.

Author's Note

The ideas for the four central elements in this novel—the tree, the church, the wounded veteran, and the tempestuous nature of Josiah Gideon—came from other books.

The tree is an American chestnut (*Castanea dentata*), but it was inspired by an ancient British chestnut (*Castanea sativa*) in Thomas Pakenham's *Meetings with Remarkable Trees*.

There are photographs of many simple rural churches in *Wooden Churches: A Celebration,* by Rick Bragg, including a church turned movie house in Woodville, Mississippi.

A magnificent volume of medical history, *Plastic Surgery of the Face,* by Sir Harold Gillies, is a photographic record of this surgeon's heroic efforts to repair facial injuries suffered by British soldiers in World War I. It provided painful information about cases like that of James Jackson Shaw.

Anthony Trollope's pugnacious clergyman, Josiah Crawley, was kidnapped from the pages of *The Last Chronicle of Barset,* set down in a New England village, and renamed Josiah Gideon.

The photographs of the nineteenth-century characters in this book came from the collection of Henry Deeks in Maynard, Massachusetts. Finding their likenesses was like moving through throngs of men, women, and children, looking for the right faces. Three of them had to resemble the characters in an earlier book but seem five years older. Amazingly, they turned up. I recognized Ida at once, and pulled her out of the crowd, along with Alexander and Eben.

As for Jack and Jacob Spratt, the only research for their aerial adventures was a breathtaking flight over the town of Queechee, Vermont, in Gary Lovell's hot-air balloon.

The town of Nashoba is fictional, forcibly squeezed into the map of Middlesex County. And although Dr. Oliver Wendell Holmes often wrote about very large trees, he had nothing whatever to say about the great chestnut of Nashoba.

For advice and counsel about trees, I'm grateful to Dr. Anne Myers, who sent me a photograph of a small North Carolina church built in 1913 of American chestnut, proving that such a building was possible. Other knowledgeable advisers about trees and sawmills were Dr. Willard Weeks of Amherst, Tom Kelleher of Old Sturbridge Village, Norman Levey of Lincoln, archivist Sheila Connor of the Arnold Arboretum, Dennis Collins of Mount Auburn Cemetery, Lincoln's Ted Tucker with his axes and grindstone, and Kim Johnson with his backyard sawmill.

Professor Robert Gross of the University of Connecticut loaned important chapters from his forthcoming book, *The Transcendentalists and Their World.* Another Thoreauvian, Professor Nikita Pokrovsky of the University of Moscow, chivvied my computer files into shape. Peggy Marsh and Ellen Raja of Lincoln improved my fragmentary understanding of nineteenth-century ways of doing things, Lincoln reference librarian Jeanne Bracken found books far and near, and my old friend Wendy

Davis invited me to a Quaker meeting in the venerable Friends Meeting House of Henniker, New Hampshire. Her daughter, Marcia Davis, drove us from one New Hampshire church to another, all of them *as simple as barns and commonplace as gas stations, but of a timeless and surpassing beauty.*